CODE
NAME:

WILLIAM W.
JOHNSTONE

PINNACLE BOOKS

Kensington Publishing Corp.

http://www.pinnaclebooks.com

PINNACLE BOOKS are published by

Kensington Publishing Corp.
850 Third Avenue
New York, NY 10022

All Kensington Titles, Imprints, and Distributed Lines
are available at special quantity discounts for bulk pur-
chases for sales promotions, premiums, fund-raising, and
educational or institutional use. Special book excerpts or
customized printings can also be created to fit specific
needs. For details, write or phone the office of the
Kensington special sales manager: Kensington Publishing Corp., 850 Third Avenue, New York, NY 10022, attn:
Special Sales Department, Phone: 1-800-221-2647.

First Printing: May 2001
10 9 8 7 6 5 4 3 2 1

Printed in the United States of America

ONE

1980

Just off the coast of Beirut, on the emerald green water of the Mediterranean, a rusting freighter rode at anchor under the noonday sun. When the bilge pumps kicked in, a stream of water started spewing from the discharge pipe, giving the illusion of some great beast of the sea relieving itself.

A ship-to-shore water taxi met John Barrone at the freighter and ferried him across the harbor. As it approached the docks, the water changed from a clear sparkling green to a dirty brown sludge. The boat operator steered around something that was floating in the water. John thought it was an automobile tire, but as it drifted by the boat, close astarboard, he saw that it was a dog, dead and bloated. The sight of a dead dog floating in the harbor didn't surprise him. All life was cheap in Beirut, including human life.

As the water taxi approached the wharf, John stood up, steadying himself against the rocking of the boat. The operator killed the engine and allowed the craft to drift the rest of the way. John grabbed one of the access ladders to stop the boat, then stepped up onto the bottom rung.

"Twenty-one, six, sixty-five Shari Umar ad Daag," the boat operator said as John started up to the top of the pier. Until that moment, John had assumed the water taxi was just one of many plying the harbor. He knew now that it wasn't by chance that the water taxi had come to the ship looking for a fare. This particular taxi had been waiting specifically for him, and its operator was John's contact. What the boat operator had given him was a street address.

Without answering, John nodded, climbed to the top, then walked to a taxi that stood less than fifty feet from the ladder, its back door already open.

"It is a nice day today," the driver said. "I hope our weather holds."

"If it does not, my trip will not be spoiled," John replied. This was the sign and countersign. John had just connected with his second contact. In the cellular concept of operatives, each contact would know only what he was required to know. The taxi driver knew to pick up John, but he didn't know where to go. John gave him the address he had received from the boat operator.

The city of Beirut was divided into several enclaves, each defended by its own army of zealots, representing such factions as the Kataeb, the Tiger Militia, Guardians of the Cedars, Zghorta, Lebanese National Resistance Front, Murabitun, Amal, and Hizb Ullah. Pickup trucks in various states of repair, most of them sporting mounted guns and filled with armed soldiers, patrolled the streets.

The taxi was unmolested during the first part of its transit. The driver, making sure it would stay that way, sped across the various zones. Through his window in the backseat, John looked out onto what could only be described as a war zone. Many of the buildings had been destroyed, and there were huge piles of rock and brick in every block. Even those buildings that hadn't been turned into rubble showed extensive damage. Most were smoke-blackened, many had windows broken or missing, and artillery fire had left several gaping holes in the brick walls.

As they left one area and crossed the border into another, a truck, mounting a brace of 40-millimeter guns, suddenly pulled out of an alley. It blocked the road and the guns were brought to bear on the taxi, forcing it to stop. One of the armed militiamen started toward the taxi.

"What is this group?" John asked.

"This is the Hizb Ullah," the driver said. "Be careful of them. They are one of the worst."

"What do they want?"

"They will ask to see your papers," the driver explained. "But it means nothing. They have no official status. They just want to show who is in charge in this neighborhood. Do nothing to anger them."

"Don't worry about that. I'll be Mr. Congeniality," John promised.

John rolled the window down and smiled up at the militiaman as he approached.

"Are you American?" the armed man asked.

"I'm Canadian," John lied. Though he wasn't Canadian, he had a Canadian passport to verify his claim.

"What is your business in Beirut?"

"I am in the import-export business."

"Passport."

John folded a fifty-dollar U.S. note inside the passport, then handed it to the militiaman. The militiaman opened the passport, saw the bill, then looked up harshly at John. "This is American money," he said, tapping the bill with a stubby forefinger.

John shrugged his shoulders. "Yes, it is," he replied. "As a Canadian it pains me to say it, but the American dollar is stronger than ours."

The militiaman looked over his shoulder at the others. When he was sure he wasn't being observed, he slipped the fifty-dollar bill into his pocket. Then he handed the passport back to John and stepped away from the taxi. He waved to the driver of the truck and the truck backed up, allowing the taxi through.

At 21665 Shari Umar ad Daaq, John met his team, consisting of four Israelis and two Lebanese. Although all six had military experience, they were now civilians hired for this operation, as was John, by a very wealthy American. As prearranged, John gave each of them access numbers to their own private Swiss bank accounts. A telephone call verified that fifty thousand dollars had been placed into each account. That was the agreed-upon fee.

The American who had contracted for their services owned an international investment and banking company called Quantum Dynamics. Four of his employees, three men and one woman, had been taken hostage by the "Party of God's Deprived," an extremist Islamic group. This had happened at the same time the Iranian students had taken over the American Embassy in Teheran. The U.S. Government was so obsessed with the embassy problem in Iran that they were unable, or unwilling, to deal with a few private citizens being held captive in Beirut.

When the American businessman realized that

he could not count on help from the government, he took matters into his own hands. A few discreet questions convinced him that John Barrone was the man he wanted to head up the rescue operation. The fact that John was a member of the CIA didn't get in the way. The businessman had contacts in high places, so he simply arranged for John to take a leave of absence from the Company.

John had never worked with any of the members of this particular opteam before, and he knew that he would never work with them again. On an ultra-deep cover mission of this sort, that was often the best policy.

"All right, now that you have all been paid, let's get down to business," John said to his men. "Do we know where they are being held?"

"We know where they were as of ten o'clock this morning," David Bin-Yishai replied. Bin-Yishai, a former Israeli colonel, was John's second in command. He opened a folder and pulled out a glossy eight-by-ten photograph. The picture he produced was a satellite image of the city of Beirut.

"How did you get this?" John asked.

"Our benefactor provided it," Bin-Yishai replied. "It is nice to have friends, and satellites, in high places," he added with a chuckle.

The picture was of the Hamra district of West Beirut, and though it was taken from an orbiting body in space, the buildings were as clear and distinct as if it had been taken from a low-flying aircraft.

"Do you see here, where Tariq Saib Salam crosses Shari Kamil Shamal?" Bin-Yishai asked, pointing to the street intersection. He handed John a magnifying glass. "Look here, at the second building from the left. The terrorists occupy this

entire building, but we believe the hostages are being kept upstairs."

"What kind of security?" John asked.

"They have guards posted out front and more
inside. They also have someone with the hostages
at all times, and these people have sworn to die
before they turn the hostages over."

"Sworn to die, have they?" John said. "Then
let's see what we can do to allow these gentlemen
to fulfill their destiny."

For the next hour, John and the others planned
the mission. Using the satellite photo, they were
able to trace the alleys and roads along their twisting paths, thus establishing the best possible approach routes. The pictures provided such detail
that they could even plan the final assault.

31545 Tang Saib Salam,
Temporary Command Headquarters,
Party of God's Deprived

One of the biggest surprises the terrorists had
received when they captured the hostages was the
discovery that the person in charge of Quantum
Dynamic's Beirut office was a woman. Even before
the raid, they knew the name, Casey Northington,
but they had no idea that Casey could be a
woman's name.

This was proof, they told each other, if proof
were needed, of the moral decadence and societal
dysfunction of American culture. What sort of people would put a woman in charge of men, especially in a city like Beirut where all Americans were
at risk? Perhaps if they had known beforehand that
the office head was female, they would have made

alternate plans. But once the mission was under way it was too late to change.

The woman hostage disturbed Mehdi al Ahmed. She was in her mid-forties, fully as old as Ahmed's own mother, and yet she made no effort to cloak her sexual appeal. On the contrary, she played up her attractiveness by bleaching her hair and painting her face and wearing provocative clothing.

Ahmed felt that her appearance was inappropriate for any woman, but especially for one as old as this one. She should be dressed in veil and sari, preferably of a dark and unobtrusive color. She should be all but invisible when one passed her on the street.

This woman certainly wasn't like that. Most disturbing of all, however, was the fact that Ahmed found himself physically attracted to her. He felt a sense of guilt over that temptation, because she was an infidel, an immodest whore who obviously reveled in her carnal nature. She also had a disrespectful attitude, and she swore like a man.

As Ahmed looked at the four prisoners in his charge, he repeatedly slid open and shut the bolt on his AK-47, though only partially so, not enough to eject a shell.

"Please stop doing that," one of the hostages said.

Ahmed looked at the one who spoke to him, but he didn't answer. Neither did he stop sliding the bolt back and forth.

"That is very annoying," the hostage said.

Ahmed ignored him.

"Hey, Omar, I have to pee," the woman said.

"My name is not Omar."

"I have to pee," the woman said again.

"You must wait," Ahmed said.

"Wait? I can't wait. I have to go now."

"We have no women to go with you."

"Well, hell, Omar, why don't you go with me? The way you have been jerking off with that gun, you might get a thrill out of watching me pee."

The other hostages laughed.

"What is jerking off?"

One of the hostages made a motion as if masturbating, and all of them laughed again, including the woman.

"You are insulting me?" Ahmed said angrily. "Don't you know that your life is in my hands?"

"No, it isn't," the woman said easily. "You are a peon, Omar. You can't do jack-shit unless your superior tells you you can. And from what I can determine, everyone here is your superior."

Ahmed's face went purple with rage, and a blood vessel began to throb visibly in his temple.

"Casey, maybe you'd better back off a little," one of the other hostages said.

"Don't tell me what to do, Bill. This little pissant may have you frightened, but not me," the woman answered. She looked at Ahmed again. "So, Omar, do you let me go pee, or do I squat right here?"

"You are Satan's whore," Ahmed said.

"And you are Allah's faggot."

Furious at her words, Ahmed stood up so quickly that the chair he had been sitting on fell over. "Woman, you have gone too far! You have defiled Allah, and I am going to—"

At that exact moment there was a loud explosion downstairs, followed by a long burst of machine-gun fire.

Three of Ahmed's comrades burst into the room.

"The Americans are here!" one of them shouted.

The leader of the group assigned one hostage to

each person, separating them so that rescue would be more difficult. "Ahmed, you stay with the woman," he ordered.

"Yes," Ahmed said.

"And remember," the leader told all of them. "Do not surrender your prisoner! It is better to kill your prisoner and yourself than to surrender them."

"Allah is Great!" Ahmed shouted.

"Allah is Great!" the others answered as they left with their own prisoners.

Ahmed was now alone with Casey Northington.

Even as the gunfire and explosions were going on all around him, Ahmed felt no personal fear. On the contrary, he found the present circumstances so exciting as to be erotically stimulating. He had never been more sexually aroused in his entire life.

Casey was an exceptionally astute woman, and she realized that the dynamics had changed. For the first time since she had been taken hostage, Ahmed actually had the power of life and death over her. And she knew, even before Ahmed knew, what he was going to do.

"No," she said in a quiet voice. "Ahmed, you don't want to do this."

"Oh, so now it is Ahmed. What happened to Omar?" Ahmed taunted.

The gunfire was inside the house. It was close, loud, very fierce, and moving up the stairs, coming closer.

"Casey Northington!" someone shouted. "Casey, if you can hear me, tell me where you are!"

"I'm in here!" Casey called. "I'm at the top of the stairs!"

Pointing his gun at her, Ahmed squeezed off a short burst of automatic fire. Blood and brain matter spewed from the back of Casey's head, like lava from an erupting volcano. Then, an amazing thing happened. At the exact moment Casey died, Ahmed experienced the most intense orgasm he had ever known.

When John kicked in the door to the room where he had heard Casey's voice, he saw a man climbing through the window. He managed to get off only one shot before the man was gone. John started toward the window, but stopped when he saw Casey lying on the floor.

"Oh, shit, no," John said quietly. From the way Casey was lying, and from the amount of blood on and around her body, John knew she was dead. Still, he had to make absolutely certain, because if there was the slightest chance that she was alive, if it came down to a choice between first aid for her or killing the man who had just shot her, he would tend to Casey.

A quick check validated his first opinion. She was dead.

"Shit!" John shouted, frustrated that he had lost one of the hostages in the rescue attempt. The fact that it was both a female and the senior-ranking hostage made his frustration even greater.

John ran to the window and looked out, first down into the alley, then up toward the roof. He didn't see anyone. Whoever murdered Casey had gotten away with it.

"John, we're secure!" Bin-Yishai shouted, bursting into the room. "Seven terrorists down, all hostages safe."

"Not all safe," John said grimly, turning back into the room from the window.

"Oh, bloody hell," Bin-Yishai said when he saw Casey. "What a cowardly thing to do."

"You want to know the worst part of it? I didn't even get a look at the face of the son of a bitch who killed her," John said.

In the distance they could hear the honking-geese sound of approaching police vehicles.

"We'd better get out of here," Bin-Yishai suggested. "Remember, we aren't operating on any governmental authority."

"Right," John agreed. "Let's go."

As he and Bin-Yishai clattered back down the stairs, John had to step over the bodies of the two terrorists he had killed on the way up. There were three more bodies downstairs, and two out front.

"Where is Casey?" one of the hostages asked as John and Bin-Yishai joined the others.

"She didn't make it," John replied.

"You mean you got her killed?" the hostage asked in a flash of anger.

"Bill, ease up. You've no call to say that," one of the other hostages said.

"The hell I don't," Bill answered. "We would have been better off if they had stayed away and let the government negotiate our release. I hope you are sorry," he added to John.

"Yeah, I am sorry," John replied. "If I had been given a choice, it would be you up there, not her. Now come on, let's get out of here."

By the time John, his team, and the former hostages got outside, the street was crowded with on-lookers who had gathered to see what was going on. Hiding in the crowd was Mehdi al Ahmed. Ahmed watched the team and the hostages get into three yellow-and-blue Renaults. He studied the faces of all of them. He was sure that two of them were Lebanese. They would be the easiest to find, and to kill. At first, he thought the others were Israeli, but now he believed the leader was an American.

"John! John Barrone! We are ready to go!" one of the others shouted.

Ahmed smiled. An American named John Barrone, he thought.

John was the last one in, and as soon as he closed the door behind him, the cars drove off. Immediately after they left, the police cars arrived. The only thing left for the police to do was disperse the crowd, and this they did with a vengeance.

As Ahmed left the scene, his mind was awash with violent and conflicting emotions. He felt anger that their holy mission had been thwarted, and he felt sadness for his fellow patriots who had died in the fight. But the strongest sensation of all was the residual intensity of the orgasm he had experienced when he killed the American woman.

He knew that was something he would have to feel again.

TWO

Twenty years later,
Parasail Pictures,
Hollywood, California

"In the movie industry," Tony Sarducci liked to say to anyone who would listen, "image is everything."

Sarducci believed it was as important for film executives to look good as it was for the actors, and to that end he spent a great deal of time, effort, and money. His weight was controlled by workouts in the gym, and his perfect tan was maintained by frequent trips to the tanning salon. His hair and nails were professionally maintained, and his perfectly capped, very white teeth cost nearly as much as a new car. He also dressed the part, with very expensive suits, silk shirts, gold chains, and hand-tooled boots.

Tony Sarducci was sitting at his desk, tapping a letter opener against the palm of his left hand. The letter opener was shaped like an aircraft propeller blade. An inscription on one of the blades read: "To Tony Sarducci from the cast and crew of *Cloud Busters.*" As he played with the letter opener, he was using the speakerphone, talking to an investor in London.

Sitting across the desk from Sarducci was his assistant, Anton Natas. In contrast to Sarducci's golden tan, Natas was pasty white. His eyes were watery blue and his hair was sparse and blond.

"I don't understand," Sarducci was saying. "You told me the money was already deposited in the London bank, that it was just a matter of getting the signatures in place so I could start drawing on the account. Now is the money in the bank, or isn't it?"

"The money is in the bank," the investor replied.

"Then put the signatures through. Based on your word to me, I started the picture and I have run up a considerable debt. I need the money, and I need it now."

"Well, that's where we are running into some difficulty," the English investor explained. "You see, some of our chaps are concerned that your TV series isn't going to be picked up."

"TV series? What the hell does the TV series have to do with our project?" Sarducci asked. "We're talking about a theatrical release here. *Colorado Outlaw* is a feature-length Western; it has nothing to do with the TV series.

"But it all goes to credibility, old man, don't you see?" the investor replied. "We convinced our European partners to invest in the picture on the strength of your having a successful television series. I can't tell you how disappointing it was when we learned that your series was not going to be picked up."

"Yeah, well, you should have seen it from my end," Sarducci replied. "But I still don't see what one has to do with the other."

"I know, you are an artist and not a business-man," the investor said. "But the bottom line, as we number-crunchers are wont to say, is that the money won't be forthcoming. I've been instructed not to release the account to you. If you can get some renewed interest in your TV series, then do get in contact with us again."

"If I had the money from the TV series, I wouldn't need you, you Limey asshole!" Sarducci shouted angrily into the speakerphone. He broke the connection before the Englishman could answer.

"That's a tough break," Natas said.

"I'm dead," Sarducci said quietly. He sighed, and sat there for a long moment, continuing to tap the letter opener in the palm of his left hand.

"I'm over a million dollars in the hole," he continued. "If I don't come up with the money by Friday, production of *Colorado Outlaw* is going to come to a halt and the lawsuits are going to start. When that happens, I'll lose all credibility. You know as well as I do, Natas, in this business credibility is everything."

"What about the studio?"

Sarducci looked around his office, as if appraising it. "I may have a million dollars equity here, I'm not sure," he said. "Whatever I have won't be enough to escape foreclosure. I'm going to lose everything."

"Maybe not," Natas said.

"I'd like to know how I'm going to avoid it."

"I have some business associates who might be able to help."

"You do?" Sarducci asked, his eyes reflecting a glimmer of hope. "Who are they? When can I meet them?"

Natas shook his head. "You won't meet them.

They are the type of people who prefer to remain anonymous."

"Why is that?"

"It goes to the type of productions they want to do."

Sarducci looked confused. "I don't understand. What kind of productions?"

"Adult videos," Natas replied.

"Porn films?" Sarducci replied. "Shit, Natas, I don't want to do that. I've had enough of a struggle just trying to garner respect for the low-budget pictures I've been doing. If I start doing porn, where will that leave me?"

"It will leave you rich," Natas said.

Sarducci chuckled. "How do you figure that?"

"Simple. The average cost of production for an adult video is fifty thousand dollars. The average income from one video is one million dollars."

Sarducci looked surprised. "The hell you say?"

"I do say."

"I had no idea the numbers were that good."

"It wouldn't take you long to get back on your feet if you did a few of those."

"No, it wouldn't, would it?" Sarducci replied.

"You could make some great adult videos," Natas said.

"You know, that's right. I mean, if a person brought some creative integrity to those films, if you used good production techniques and not just a handheld camera and a mattress on a basement floor somewhere, you could give these films real artistic value," Sarducci said.

"Absolutely," Natas agreed.

"I mean, after all, look at literature. Almost every novel you read now is filled with very graphically described sex scenes. And yet they are legitimate best-sellers, reviewed by *The New York Times,* read by the best people, and discussed openly at cocktail parties."

"That's true," Natas said.

"Why shouldn't the motion picture business have the same freedom and the same legitimacy as literature?"

"There is no reason why not," Natas said.

"The first thing we are going to have to do is change the public perception of the adult film industry. I've seen a few of the adult videos they are making today, and in every one of them the actors and actresses look hard, used, worn out. Whenever possible, I think I would like to use new, fresh faces. In fact, I could recruit them myself."

"Good idea."

"I hear that the adult film industry has its own awards ceremonies every year," Sarducci said.

"That's true. It's just like winning an Oscar," Natas said.

"These associates of yours. They would be willing to pay off my debt and finish *Colorado Outlaw?*"

Natas shook his head. "You will have to drop *Colorado Outlaw,*" he said. "But they will pay off the debt so you can keep a share of the studio."

"A share?"

"I'm sure they will want a percentage."

"How much of a percentage?"

"Forty-nine percent. That will still leave you with fifty-one percent. They don't want to control it, you understand. They just want to make a profit from their investment."

Sarducci stroked his chin for a long moment. Natas had said that the arrangement would leave him fifty-one percent. In truth, this deal would only leave him forty-nine percent for he had, long ago, given two percent to Wanda Carmody, his secretary of the last twenty years. On the other hand, he would effectively have fifty-one percent because he knew that Wanda would vote however he asked her to.

"I think the first thing I want to do is change the name of the company," Sarducci said. "I wouldn't want Parasail Pictures associated with adult films. I mean, I'm perfectly willing to do them, but I think I should keep Parasail out of it."

"I'm sure my associates would have no problem with that," Natas replied. "All they want is to be able to get a foot in the production door. You can call it whatever you wish."

Sarducci thought for a moment, then smiled. "I'm going to call it Wet Spot Productions."

Natas laughed. "Excellent choice. Not only in the name of the company, but also in your agreeing to the arrangement. You are going to make a lot of money, Sarducci. More than you have ever made before."

"You understand that even though I am going to dedicate myself to making this business as respectable as possible, my first love is, and will always be, for the more traditional films."

"I do understand," Natas said.

"Call your associates," Sarducci said. "Tell them they have a deal."

Code Name Team Headquarters,
Southwestern U.S.

The entire Code Name Team was gathered for a type of homecoming. Wagner liked to do this from time to time, not only as a means of disseminating information and orders, but also as a way of enabling everyone to relax.

Their gathering place was so secret and unapproachable that they sometimes referred to it as Area Fifty-Two, a takeoff on the top-secret Area Fifty-One. There were very few people who knew about the Code Name Team, fewer still who knew what it was, and only the most trusted who could name its members.

The Code Name Team was an extra-legal rather than illegal group. Its job was to "handle" things that fell through the cracks of legal technicality. The team was created to take care of the dregs of society; those terrorists, murderers, drug-dealers, etc., who too often got away with their misdeeds because of misguided liberal guilt over the normal inequities of nature.

Although the Code Name Team had no connection with the government, there were a few highly placed individuals in the government who knew, and privately appreciated, what the team was doing. To that end, they managed to turn a blind eye to the team's operations.

Because of the supersecret nature of the team, its members had no family or social life. They had no future and they had burned the bridges to their past. There was more than one way into the team, but there was no way out, short of a body bag. The men and women of the Code Name Team were teammates, coworkers, fellow warriors, friends, and family in and of themselves.

Those few times they were able to come together without a specific assignment were rare, and when they did come together, they managed to find ways to unwind and relax.

As two dozen Kansas City prime steaks were

cooking over a mesquite fire, several members of the team were out on the patio, kicked back in lawn chairs, drinking cold beer and looking up into the sky.

"Who came up with this crazy idea anyway?" John Barrone asked.

"It was Mike Rojas's idea," Jenny Barnes answered.

"Hey, don't blame me," the big Mexican American replied. "I just challenged them, that's all. I didn't know they would actually take me up on it."

Wagner had come out of the house just in time to hear the last few sentences of conversation. Although Wagner wasn't a field operative, he was a member of the team in that he was the contact between the consortium that funded them and approved of their missions and the field operatives themselves. The other team members respected Wagner and were friendly toward him. But he didn't face the same dangers they did, so no matter how friendly they were, he was never really one of them.

"What are you talking about?" Wagner asked.

"Nothing really," Paul Brewer answered. Paul was the only black member of the team. He still had the build and athletic grace of the professional football player he once was, and like the others, he was looking toward the sky.

Wagner looked up as well, but he wasn't wearing his sunglasses, so the brightness of the clear blue sky caused his eyes to water.

"Anyhow, if it doesn't work, you will find out soon enough," Chris Farmer said.

"If what doesn't work?" Wagner asked.

"The exchange."

"The exchange? Will someone please give me some straight information?"

"Oh, Lana and Linda are going to try and make a parachute exchange," Bob Garrett said.

Wagner was as confused as before.

"Yes, well, you know how Lana and Linda are," Jenny told him. "They are always trying to prove something."

"And they are very competitive," Paul said.

They continued to stare into the sky.

Wagner looked around. "Where are they?" he asked.

"Where is who?" John asked.

"Well, who are we talking about? Linda Marsh and Lana Henry. Where are they?"

"Hey, folks, the steaks are done," Don Yee said. "Are we going to eat, or what?"

"We'll eat after the parachute exchange," John said.

"Where are Linda and Lana?" Wagner asked. "Maybe they can explain what's going on."

"Listen, I think I'll just sort of have one of these steaks now, and maybe another later, if you all don't mind," Don said, spearing one of the steaks from the grill. He tossed it from hand to hand for a moment, blowing on it, until it was cool enough, then took a bite from it, eating it as he would a piece of bread.

"I think that's them," Chris said matter-of-factly.

"Yeah, I see them," Paul said.

Wagner looked up again, and this time he saw what everyone was looking at. Two small dots, high in the sky. Higher yet was the airplane they had jumped from.

"Good Lord, is that them?" he said. "I didn't know they were sky divers."

"Actually, I don't think either one of them has ever made a jump before," Chris said.

"And you talked them into jumping?" Wagner asked Mike Rojas.

"Well, not exactly," Mike replied. "What I talked them into was switching parachutes."

"Yes, you said that, but I still don't understand what you mean."

"Well, it's simple really," Jenny said. "The idea is to jump out of the airplane not wearing their parachutes but holding them. Then, as they are free-falling, they will exchange parachutes, put them on, then pull the rip cord."

"That's all there is to it," Paul said.

"What?" Wagner gasped. "Why, that is the most preposterous thing I have ever heard. Who would do such a dumb thing? I'm not even sure it can be done."

"Oh, it can be done, all right," Jenny said.

"How do you know?"

"Because Paul and I did it yesterday."

"One of the chutes just opened," Don said.

Overhead they saw a chute open, spreading red and white against the sky, slowing the descent of the jumper, though from this distance they had no idea who it was. The other jumper continued to fall.

"Why doesn't *that* chute open?" Wagner asked.

"One person is almost always going to be a little behind the other," Jenny explained. "Besides, you are going to want a little distance between you when the chutes open."

The jumper continued to plunge earthward, no longer a dot, but the arms and legs clearly visible now, so that it could easily be identified as a person.

"I think that's Lana," Chris said. He was looking through a pair of binoculars.

"Can you tell what she is doing? Is she having trouble?" Wagner asked.

"Seems to be," Chris said easily. "She can't get the chute on."

"Oh, shit!" Wagner said anxiously.

"Don, toss me another beer, would you?" John asked casually.

"Sure thing," Don replied. He fished a beer from the cooler, then tossed it over to John. John pulled open the pop-tab and when he did, some of the beer spewed onto Jenny. Shouting in alarm, she moved quickly to get out of the spray. The others laughed.

"Lana can't get her chute open and you people are just playing around down here. You're crazy!" Wagner said.

"You're calling *us* crazy?" Paul asked, pointing to Lana's plummeting body. "Figure it out. *She's* the one trying to put on a parachute."

"My God!" Wagner said. He put his hands to the side of his head. "My God!"

Less than five hundred feet overhead the chute suddenly blossomed. A second later the sound of its opening, like the pop of a whip, reached them.

"Oh, thank God, thank God," Wagner said, thoroughly shaken by the entire episode.

"Have a beer, Mr. Wagner," John said, handing him an open can.

"No, thanks, I don't care for one," Wagner replied, lifting the can to his mouth with a shaking hand and taking a long, Adam's-apple-bobbing drink.

"Let's eat," Don Yee said. "I'm starving." Licking his fingers to get rid of the last of the steak he had just consumed, Don was the first in line to go through the buffet.

As they ate, Lana was teased about being a klutz and butterfingers for taking so long to get her chute on. She took the good-natured teasing in stride.

"Well, even if you had hit, you wouldn't have been that hard to clean up," Bob said. "Hell, you aren't that big a girl."

The others laughed at Bob's black humor. All but Wagner. When Jenny looked over toward their assignments manager, she saw that Wagner was still pale over the prospect of nearly seeing Lana killed in the fall.

"Buck up, Wagner," Jenny said. "Don't you know that there is nobody, anywhere, who gives a shit whether any of us lives or dies?"

"That's wrong," Wagner said seriously. "I give a shit."

The others lifted their beers to him in salute, because they realized that what he had just told them was true. He did give a shit.

Hollywood

"Sarducci has agreed to the deal," Natas told his business partner. "We are going to start shooting right away."

"I don't know. I still think we should have asked for fifty-one percent," the big man replied.

Natas shook his head. "No. In the first place, I doubt he would have gone along with it if he had thought we were going to take controlling interest. And in the second place, by letting him keep controlling interest, he will be the designated go-to-jail person if some of our more creative activities are compromised."

The big man laughed. "The designated go-to-jail guy," he said. "I like that."

"So, it looks like you've come up in the world," Natas said. "You've gone from squeezing whores and pimps for protection money to being a movie mogul."

"Yeah, how about that? Hey, what do you think? Should I get one of those chairs? You know, those tall canvas chairs with the word 'Director' on the back?"

"I think you should provide the muscle, and leave the movie business to us," Natas said.

"The muscle *and* the money," the big man added. "Don't forget where your financing came from."

THREE

When the big Lincoln slowed, Tulip moved toward the curb. Denied the windbreak of the building, she felt a chill as the cool breeze whipped around her bare legs and under her micro-miniskirt. It had rained earlier, and now the nipples of her small but well-formed breasts were standing out in bold relief against her damp T-shirt. When she approached the limo, she affected a smile as the shaded window slid down. A middle-aged man with a round red face and very thick glasses looked up at her.

"Well, now, aren't you a handsome fellow, though?" Tulip quipped, turning slightly and thrusting a hip provocatively toward the car.

"How old are you?" the driver asked.

"Old enough to know what it's all about," Tulip answered flippantly. She licked her lips.

"How old?" the man asked again.

"Nineteen," Tulip lied. She was seventeen, but she needed this trick because she wanted to get off the street. Whoever said it didn't get cold in Los

Angeles had obviously never stood out on a cool damp night with the wind whirling around their nearly bare ass.

"You're nineteen? You don't look it."

"I am, really. And I have a driver's license to prove it."

The round-faced man stroked his cheek for a moment as he studied her. What he saw was a thin, young girl with eyes that were much older than her years.

Tulip didn't wither under his scrutiny. She had been on the streets for nearly a month now, and she knew that this was part of the process.

Finally the man sighed. "Too bad. I didn't think you were that old. I want someone young." Without another word, the dark-tinted window slid back up and the Lincoln drove away.

"Young? Wait a minute! Are you saying I'm too old for you?" Tulip shouted at the car as it pulled away. "Why, you decrepit old fart! I bet you haven't had a hard-on in thirty years!"

Angry and frustrated by the rejection, Tulip walked back to the relative shelter of the building and the residual warmth of the bricks that were slowly giving back the heat they had absorbed during the day.

Bunny laughed. "First time you've ever run across Uncle Billy?"

Tulip looked back at the young black girl who was sharing the corner with her tonight. "That old fool's name is Uncle Billy?"

"Well, that's what he wants the girls to call him. The very young girls, that is. How old did you tell him you were?"

"Nineteen."

"You should have told him you were fifteen. If

I had seen who it was in time, I could've told you. He likes them young."

"And here I thought I was too young for him."

"Oh, honey, for someone like that, you can't be too young," Bunny said. "If you had told him you were fifteen, that little ole pecker of his would have popped out of his pants."

Tulip laughed at the image. "Now you tell me."

A bright red Dodge Ram pickup truck drove by. On top of the truck was a light bar. On the back window was a Confederate flag, a translucent decal that could be seen, but seen through. When the pickup reached the far end of the block it slowed, then turned around and started back.

"Here comes my john," Bunny said.

"I don't know about that. Did you see the flag on the back window? He's probably got pig shit on his boots."

"Trust me, honey," Bunny said. "Sometimes, the redder their necks are, the more they like their brown sugar."

Bunny walked out to the curb and struck a pose. The pickup truck stopped, there was a moment of negotiation, then Bunny got inside. When the truck drove away, Bunny turned, and looking through the translucent flag on the rear window, flashed a smile and a wave.

As the drone of the truck engine disappeared, it was replaced by the moan of the wind. At this time of night Sunset Boulevard was quiet, and Tulip suddenly realized that she was the only girl left. She felt very much alone, and when she shivered, it wasn't entirely from the chill.

A flash of headlights caught her attention, and as she looked up the street she saw a shining black Mercedes coming toward her. The car glided to a stop, and the right front window was lowered. When Tulip bent over to look inside the car, she saw a man in his mid-thirties, dripping with gold chains and earrings. Unlike the round-faced pedophile, this man was tanned, trim, and handsome. Tulip's smile became genuine. She wanted very much to get off the street tonight, and it would be a pleasant bonus to do so with a man who was not only closer to her own age, but also fairly good-looking. A little nagging thought in the back of her mind made her wonder why someone like this would have to be paying for his women, but she let the thought die.

"Hello," she said as seductively as possible.

"Hello yourself," the john replied. He looked at her for a moment. "Would you mind turning around for me?"

"Beg your pardon?"

The john held out his right hand and made a circling motion. As he did so, the huge diamond on his ring finger glistened brightly in the ambient light. "Turn around for me," he said. "Pirouette."

Feeling just a little foolish, Tulip did as he requested.

"Yes," the john said. "You'll do nicely."

Tulip chuckled. "I've never been asked to"—she paused for a second, setting the next word apart—"pirouette—before."

"You've probably never been asked if you would like to star in a movie before either."

"A movie? What is this? You trying to talk me into something? You don't have to talk me into anything, mister. All you have to do is pay me. I'm a working girl. If I go with you, it's going to cost you."

"Oh, I'm perfectly prepared to pay you, my dear. And pay you quite well. How does twenty-five hundred dollars sound?"

"Are you serious? Are you really a movie producer?" Tulip grinned broadly. " 'Cause if you are, that's why I came out here to Los Angeles in the first place. I wanted to be in movies. Like Julia Roberts. Did you see *Pretty Woman*?"

The john chuckled. "Well, now, don't get your hopes up too high. This isn't exactly a Julia Roberts–type film. In fact, it won't even be a theatrical release. It's more for private viewing, if you know what I mean."

"You mean porn film?"

"In the industry, we prefer the term 'adult film.' "

"The industry," Tulip said. "I like that. 'The industry.' That sounds real important."

"Are you interested?"

"Twenty-five hundred dollars, you say? When do I get paid?"

The john produced his wallet, then pulled out five one-hundred-dollar bills. "Five hundred right now," he said. "The other two thousand when we are finished."

"How long will it take?"

"Oh, we'll do it all in a couple of days."

"I thought movies took a long time to do."

The john laughed again. "I told you, this isn't the kind of film you will find on network TV. All you need is a camera, a mattress, and some willing bodies."

"What will I have to do?"

"Nothing you haven't already done, I'm sure." The john opened the door, and the light illuminated the soft, red leather interior. "Get in. I do believe a star is about to be born," he said with a specious smile.

"A star," Tulip said. "Yeah, I could live with that."

Two months later,
Sidewalk café,
Hollywood and Vine

The two men were sitting at a table on the patio of an upscale cafe. The subjects they were discussing—distribution, numbers, and production schedules—were no different from a hundred other similar conversations that would take place in Hollywood on that very same day. In most cases, however, such discussions would be empty of any substance, representing as they did people without money trying to make deals with other people without money. In this case, however, there was some essence to the conversation, for one man really was in the business of supplying pictures, and the other really was in the business of buying and distributing them.

"This particular type of picture cannot be made every day. I'm sure you understand the risks involved," the producer said.

"I understand," the distributor replied. "There are risks involved in distributing them as well, but those risks make the picture a desirable, and valuable, commodity."

"Your risks are not nearly as great as mine."

The distributor smiled. "If you are caught, you will face a long, drawn-out trial. If you are found guilty, you will go to prison for a while. Then you will be released. It is very different in my world. If I am caught, there will be no trial and there will be no prison. There will be only my execution by means of a public beheading."

The filmmaker snorted. "You live in a barbaric world, my friend."

"Yes. Nevertheless, I am willing to take those risks for our mutual benefit. Are you prepared to do so as well?"

"How many pictures do you want?"

The distributor smiled, then held up his thumb and forefinger. "I want two," he said.

"I will start production immediately."

"Wait," the distributor said. He took a tape from his case and handed it across the table to the filmmaker. "I want this one."

The filmmaker looked surprised. "I don't understand," he said. "You already have that one."

The distributor shook his head. "I want a different ending to this one. A special ending."

"I'm not sure I can get that actress again."

"Offer her a great deal of money. Promise her stardom," the distributor said. "I have some people who will pay a great deal of money to see her in the special ending."

"Why? Why this girl? She seems rather ordinary to me."

"Who can explain the tastes of some people?" the distributor replied. "If you change the ending, I will pay you as if you had made an entirely new picture."

The filmmaker thought for a moment, then nodded. "I will do it. But I want two million dollars. One million dollars for each tape."

The distributor drew in a sharp breath. "Two million dollars is a lot of money. Such pictures are not expensive to make."

"Yes, but you understand that these films cannot

be copyrighted, so I have no protection once I give you the masters. I know that you will copy them and make three times as much as I am asking. Perhaps even more, for your earning potential will continue for the life of the tape. I must get all of my money up front."

The distributor thought for a moment, then smiled and nodded. "I see that we understand each other," he said. "Very well, it is a deal."

"I'm glad. We have done well over the last couple of years."

"I would hope so. After all, I have entered into partnership with Satan, and I would expect no less than a handsome profit for bartering my soul."

The two men shook hands.

On the other side of the restaurant patio, a young photographer had just changed lenses on his camera. He had been hired by a magazine to do a photo-journal piece entitled "A Day in Tinseltown," an hour-by-hour account of everything that goes on in Hollywood in one day. He had started shooting early this morning. So far he had captured such images as a street-cleaner moving down a predawn, quiet street, a catering service loading their truck to take food to a movie shoot, a homeless man leaning against the front of a not-yet-open liquor store, and some children of the wealthy being delivered to school by chauffeured limousine.

Now he was intrigued by the two men on the other side of the patio, not only by the intensity of their discussion, but by the artistic image they presented. One man was exceptionally pale, whiter than anyone the photographer had ever seen before. The other man was very dark, not dark like an African American, but dark like someone from the Middle East. He snapped the picture.

FOUR

Even'song Estate,
Long Island, New York

The heart of Even'song Estate was a sixty-four-room pile, sitting in the middle of twelve acres of beautifully maintained flower gardens, mature trees, and a gently rolling lawn that ended at the water's edge on the northeast corner of Long Island. The twelve-foot-high stone fence that surrounded the estate was topped with razor wire and guarded by motion sensors, radar, and closed-circuit television. A steel crash-proof gate protected the only road onto the place, and it was manned twenty-four hours a day by armed guards who watched everything from behind bullet-proof glass.

Marist J. Quinncannon had not always lived in such a fortress. But twenty years earlier four employees of his company, Quantum Dynamics, were taken hostage in Beirut by Islamic extremists. When the U.S. Government did nothing to effect their release, the billionaire businessman took matters into his own hands, putting together a team of mercenaries to rescue his employees.

Seven terrorists and one of the hostages were killed during the operation. The fact that the dead hostage was a woman, and Quinncannon's bureau chief, did not go down well with the rest of the country, and some of the more liberal politicians even suggested that Quinncannon was guilty of murder.

Then, two years ago, the current Administration apologized to the Islamic organization that had taken Quinncannon's employees hostage, and paid twenty million dollars to the "Party of God's Deprived" in reparations for its loss of life.

In the meantime, those same extremists offered their own one-million-dollar reward to anyone who would kill Marist J. Quinncannon, a man they referred to as "The American Devil."

Publicly, the U.S. Government filed a protest. Privately, the President sent word to Quinncannon that there was nothing the government could do to protect him. What the President didn't realize was that Quinncannon not only didn't expect government help, he didn't want it. He had seen the current government in action. He would much rather protect himself.

Anyone who came to see Quinncannon did so at Quinncannon's personal invitation. John Barrone, Jennifer Barnes, and Don Yee were here as a result of one of those rare personal invitations. They had turned onto Breeze Tree Road, and Don was looking at a map of Long Island.

"You sure this is the way?" Don asked. "According to the map, there is nothing beyond this point."

"I'm sure this is the way," John said easily.

"How are you so sure?"

"I'm just sure."

"You were one of them, weren't you?" Jennifer asked.

"One of who?"

"You know who. The mercenary team that freed Quinncannon's people. You were in on that raid in Beirut twenty years ago."

"Was I?"

"In fact, if memory serves, you were the team leader."

"Impossible," John said. "I was still working for the Company then."

"Uh-huh."

The radar detector in the car beeped and flashed.

"We've just been picked up," Don said.

John chuckled. "Hardly. Quinncannon has had us under observation ever since we turned off Highway Twenty-seven."

"Are you serious? That was six miles back," Jennifer said. "Just how rich is Quinncannon to have that kind of surveillance system in place?"

"Oh, I think you will find he is rich enough to get about anything done he wants done," John answered. "Here it is."

They approached a closed gate and stopped. A camera, attached to a telescopic arm, swung down from its position on a pole on the side of the road. The camera moved slowly across the windshield of the car, stopping in front of John. As it took his picture, it also painted him with a red-line scanner. An electronic monotone voice came from its speaker.

"John Barrone, age fifty, six feet two inches tall, gray hair, blue eyes, slight astigmatism, twenty-year veteran of CIA, veteran of U.S. Marine Corps."

The camera moved to the center of the windshield then projected a laser beam into the backseat.

"Will the occupant of the backseat please move into the position indicated by the red-beam light?"

"Move, Don," John said.

Don Yee positioned himself accordingly.

"Don Yee, five feet six inches tall, Oriental, black hair, brown eyes, thirty-three years old, ten-year veteran of CIA, computer expert, fifth-degree black belt."

Once again, the camera moved until it was at the right side of the windshield, in front of Jennifer.

"Wait a minute," Jennifer said. "If this thing is going to give away my age, I'm outta here."

The two men laughed.

"Jennifer Barnes, blond hair, blue eyes, five feet four inches tall. Thirty years old, eight years with the FBI. Specialty is explosives. Female, very attractive."

"How do you like that?" Jennifer asked. "A sexist robot."

"Yeah, well, at least it has a good eye, if not good taste," John teased.

"Screw you," Jennifer said with a laugh. With a slight whirring sound, the camera pulled back from the car and the gate opened.

As the car moved up the long curving drive, Don looked at the house in awe. "Wow. This isn't a house, this is a hotel. Do we know what room Quinncannon is staying in?"

"Would you believe this is just his summer cottage?" John asked. He stopped under the portico and a tall, well-dressed gentleman with a pleasant smile stepped forward to greet them. As they got out of the car, John noticed at least four more less-conspicuous and well-armed men who weren't smiling. All business, they were focusing on any possible threat to their employer.

"I'm Phelps. Mr. Quinncannon is waiting inside. If you would come with me, please?" Phelps said.

As they passed through a wide hall lined with suits of real armor, Jennifer and Don Yee seemed more fascinated by their surroundings than did

John. Few of John's colleagues knew that he was from old money. Not as much money as enjoyed by Quinncannon, but affluence on both sides of his family had rendered him immune to intimidation by wealth.

"You'll find Mr. Quinncannon in there," Phelps said, pointing to an open door at the opposite end of the hall.

"Thanks, Phelps," John said.

The room looked as if it were a part of the New York Public Library. Bookshelves, which stretched from the floor to a twelve-foot-high ceiling, lined the room. The shelves were filled with books, and John had the distinct feeling that they weren't merely for show.

A tall man with silver hair was standing in the middle of the room. He extended his hand in greeting as the three approached him. "Mr. Barrone," he said. "So good to see you again."

Jennifer sneaked a look at Don and mouthed the word "again?"

"Mr. Quinncannon, allow me to introduce my colleagues, Miss Jennifer Barnes and Mr. Don Yee."

Quinncannon greeted them both, then invited them to sit down. Two leather chairs and a leather couch formed a seating area.

"Would you look at the TV screen, please?" Quinncannon asked. Picking up a remote, he caused a panel to slide open, revealing a large-screen TV. With another click, a tape began to play.

The video was of a young, very pretty, fresh, innocent-looking young girl in a short-skirted, green-and-yellow cheerleader's uniform. A block-letter H was on the blouse of the uniform.

Contorting herself to form the letters, the girl began to give a cheer. "*V - I - C - T - O - R - Y. Victory,*

victory is our cry. Are we in it? Well, I guess. Will we win it? Yes, yes, yes! Hawthorn, Hawthorn, HAWTHORN!"

The young girl finished the cheer with a leap, throwing her arms over her head and spreading her legs, causing her short skirt to fly up, exposing young, shapely, well-toned thighs.

Quinncannon turned off the TV.

"That is my granddaughter, Annette Quinncannon. As you may have read in the papers, one year ago my son, Jason, was killed while racing his boat. I invited my daughter-in-law and granddaughter to come live with me. Annette had some, uh, difficulty adjusting, first to her father's death and then to. . . ." Quinncannon paused.

"To the fact that Marist and I fell in love," a new voice said. The voice belonged to a woman who had just come into the room. She was in her forties, tall and attractive. As John looked at her, he saw a striking resemblance to the young girl on the videotape. The woman saw him looking at her.

"Yes, Mr. Barrone, I am Vivian Quinncannon, Jason's widow. Some may find my romantic relationship with the father of my late husband shocking, but I ask, why is it so difficult to understand? I loved Jason very much and, after all, is Marist not the original of the man I loved?"

"You say some find your relationship with your father-in-law shocking. By that, do you mean your daughter?" Jennifer asked.

Vivian walked over to stand beside Quinncannon. He took her hand in his as she looked toward the floor. "Yes," she said quietly. "My daughter is one of those who is finding the concept difficult to accept."

"Where is your daughter now?" Don asked.

"I don't know," Vivian answered. Her eyes welled with tears.

"That's why we have asked you here," Quinncannon said. He cleared his throat. "I know that the Code Name Team wasn't put together to find runaway teenage girls. But as you may or may not know, I am one of the original founders and backers of your organization. I have personally given more than one hundred million dollars to see to the success of the team's operation and—God help me—I called your man Wagner and asked for a personal favor."

John, Jennifer, and Don were silent for a moment.

Quinncannon cleared his throat. "Now that I have you here, I see that I may have overstepped the boundary." He pinched the bridge of his nose. "You've had a long drive. Please, have dinner with me and stay the night. You can return tomorrow. I won't demand anything of you."

"Marist?" Vivian said, looking down at him with a pained expression on her face.

Quinncannon put his other hand on hers and rubbed it gently.

"Vivian, if I forced them to do this, it would go against everything the Code Name Team was formed for."

"No, it wouldn't," John said. "We were formed to be of service to people, to perform in areas that are too difficult or too sensitive for any government agency."

"John is telling it like it is, Mr. Quinncannon," Jennifer said. "You have every right to ask for our help."

"We'll find her," Don said.

"Thank you, my friends," Quinncannon said. "Thank you from the bottom of my heart."

"But the dinner, that still goes, right?" Don asked.

Quinncannon laughed. "Absolutely, Mr. Yee. Just tell my chef what you want. And if you ask for it, I promise you, we will roast an elephant."

Hawthorn Academy for Young Ladies,
Long Island

The headmistress of Hawthorn Academy was a woman in her mid-forties. She had a nice shape and, with a less severe hairstyle, more flattering clothes, and a little makeup, might even have been considered attractive. Her name was Miss Joyce Bremerton, and she emphasized the "Miss" when she introduced herself.

Miss Bremerton led John into a reception room just down the hall from her own office. "You can interview Annette's classmates in here," she said. "Our parents use this room when they visit their daughters."

"Thank you, Miss Bremerton," John replied.

There had been a visiting room like this one at his kids' school too, but John had seldom used it.

After his wife, Michelle, was killed while jogging, John enrolled their two kids, John Jr. and Ellen, in a private boarding school near Washington, D.C. John's work kept him away from his kids more than he ever thought it would. He had fully intended to stay close to them, but it didn't work out that way. John Jr. and Ellen were independent and adaptable, and when they realized that he wasn't going to be there all the time, they became totally self-sufficient. At first they got along without him by necessity. Eventually, they got along without him by choice. John Jr. now worked with an advertising agency in New York, while Ellen was an attorney with a Manhattan law firm.

In the meantime the mugger who had raped Michelle, then cut her throat, was paroled after serving only eight years of his twenty-five-year prison sentence.

When Miss Bremerton returned to the visiting room with one of her students a moment later, John noticed that the woman had combed her hair and put on fresh lipstick. It was a decided improvement, and he looked pointedly at the change. He said nothing about it, but he didn't have to. Miss Bremerton knew he had noticed, and her cheeks pinked as, self-consciously, she touched her hair.

"Uh, this is Miss Audra Simmons," Miss Bremerton said.

Audra was an attractive young girl of about seventeen. Like all the other students he had seen since arriving at the school, she was wearing the academy uniform of muted green and yellow plaid skirt and a green shirt.

"Audra, this is Mr. Barrone. He would like to ask you a few questions about Annette Quinncannon."

"Is she in trouble?" Audra asked.

"I don't know," John replied. "We hope she isn't. We hope she is safe somewhere. But her mother and grandfather haven't heard from her in a long time and they are very worried about her."

"I told her that her mother would worry about her," Audra said. "I told her I would worry about her, and so would all her other friends. But she wouldn't listen to me. She was determined to go anyway."

"Go where?"

Audra didn't answer.

"Audra, do you know where Annette is?" Miss Bremerton asked.

Audra still didn't answer, but a tear began to slide down her cheek.

"Audra, this is very important," John said. "You do want to help her, don't you?"

"Annette made me swear not to tell," Audra replied.

"Is she your friend?" John asked.

"Oh, yes, she is my best friend. That's why I could never go against a promise I made to her."

"Sometimes you have to do things to help your friends, even if they don't want you to. You just have to decide which is more important, your promise to keep her secret or the need to keep her safe. If you had to choose between those two, which would it be?"

"I'd want her to be safe," Audra admitted.

John smiled at her. "You've made the right decision."

"I told her not to go out there," Audra said.

"Not to go out where?"

"Hollywood. I told her, maybe in the old days, you know, a long time ago, people could go out there and get discovered and become a movie star. But it doesn't work like that anymore."

"You think she went to Hollywood?"

Audra nodded. "I know she did. I got a postcard from her."

"Do you still have the postcard?"

Audra nodded. "It's in my room."

"Would you get it, please?" Miss Bremerton asked.

Audra nodded. "Yes, ma'am."

FIVE

Casino Monte Carlo,
Monaco

Mehdi al Ahmed stood at the window of his hotel room, looking down on the sculptured garden below. He finished the scotch he was holding, wiped his mouth with the back of his hand, then refilled his glass.

He liked scotch.

Followers of the Islamic faith weren't supposed to drink alcohol, but Ahmed truly believed that Allah had granted him special dispensation. Ahmed had to become an apostate in order to accomplish the mission he had given himself.

Twenty years ago, Ahmed was fired with religious zeal. He was then a member of the "Party of God's Deprived," the most extreme element in the fight against Western decadence. A true veteran of the revolution, Ahmed had taken part in several bombings, assassinations, and other acts of patriotism.

But it was on Teheran, Iran, not Beruit, Lebanon, that the world focused its attention when a group of students took over the American Embassy and held several diplomats hostage. In order to validate their own agenda, the leaders of the Party of God's

Deprived ordered Ahmed's group to take hostages from an American company doing business in Beirut.

That operation was ill-conceived from the beginning, when they learned that the ranking hostage was a woman. Ahmed watched every member of his group die when an international group of mercenaries rescued the American hostages. Of the special hostage unit, only Ahmed escaped death that day, and he took a vow to search out and kill every member of the rescue team.

It was to fulfill that vow that Ahmed found it necessary to adopt the decadent ways of the infidel. Only if he was one of them, only if he understood them and their evil ways, only if he could move freely among them, could he complete his sacred task.

In truth, his task was nearly done; only two men remained alive from that original rescue team. As it so happened, those two had been the leaders of the rescue team, an Israeli named David Bin-Yishai, the second in command, and the team's leader and sole American, John Barrone.

Barrone was in the United States, but David Bin-Yishai was right here in Monaco, right now. Bin-Yishai, once a colonel in the Israeli Army, now enjoyed the good life; alcohol, food, gambling, and women. He was able to enjoy that life because he was a mercenary without peer, selling his services to causes all over the world. His military expertise and thirst for action had made him a very wealthy man, and one of his greatest pleasures was spending time at the tables in Monte Carlo.

That was why Ahmed was here.

Those who had been acquainted with Ahmed in his younger days, who knew him for his religious zeal and self-righteous pride in being poor, might well wonder how he could afford to live as he now lived. What no one knew was that Ahmed had become a very wealthy man, having stumbled onto a source of immense income.

Some might say he discovered the key to wealth by accident, but Ahmed didn't believe in accidents. He believed everything had its purpose, and if the way to wealth was shown to him by Allah, then surely it was in order to provide him with the economic means he needed to complete his mission.

The fulfillment of his vow of revenge wasn't the only quest undertaken by Ahmed. After experiencing a mind-blowing orgasm at the moment of his female hostage's death, Ahmed tried, many times over the next several years, to recapture that intensity. He experimented with sadomasochism, thinking that might provide the release he sought. It was a poor substitute.

Then, while exploring the seamier side of sex, Ahmed discovered a new and very dark genre of pornographic video. This was it! This was what he had been looking for!

Ahmed became the genre's most devoted fan. He also became an international distributor when he found others who not only shared his appreciation for the genre, but were willing to pay quite handsomely to possess such tapes. Since that discovery, Ahmed had pursued the "specialty" pornographic business with an almost religious fanaticism.

His most recent visit to the United States had been exceptionally profitable, more profitable than any previous visit. In fact, he had become so wealthy through his special film distribution business that it would be very easy to give up the quest for revenge. After all, the patriotic fervor and religious passion that had once burned in him was now no more than a fading memory. That he continued his quest at all was out of a sense of obligation, not so much to his religious belief today as it was to the zeal of his youth.

It was dark when David Bin-Yishai came out of the casino. He had had a pretty good run at the tables, and had met a young woman from Holland who claimed to be a member of the Royal Family.

Bin-Yishai didn't care whether she was royalty or not; she was a pretty girl and she had accepted an invitation to spend the weekend on his boat with him. So if she wanted to call herself a princess, he was perfectly willing to let her do so.

He gave his parking ticket to the attendant, a swarthy man dressed in a red waistcoat and black trousers. Bin-Yishai had been here many times, but this was a parking lot attendant he didn't recognize.

"Where is Pierre LeGrande?" Bin-Yishai asked.

"Pierre is sick," the attendant replied. The parking attendant was about forty, small and swarthy.

"It must have come on him suddenly. He was feeling fine when I arrived this afternoon."

"Yes," the attendant said. "It was sudden. Wait here. I will get the cart and take you to your car."

"Don't bother," Bin-Yishai replied. "The walk will be good for me."

"It is no problem," the attendant replied. "It is my job."

"All right."

The attendant left for a moment, then returned with an electric cart, much like a golf cart, that the hotel used to ferry people to cars that were parked in the far corners of the lot. Bin-Yishai got in beside him, and they drove off.

The cart went down the hill, then around a curve. At this point in its route, it passed under a canopy of spreading cedar trees. Here, it was totally shielded from view. The cart stopped.

"What's wrong? Battery dead?" Bin-Yishai asked.

When the attendant turned toward him, Bin-Yishai saw that he was holding a gun in his hand. A silencer was affixed to the end of the barrel.

"What the hell?" Bin-Yishai asked. "Are you robbing me?"

"No, Colonel Bin-Yishai," Ahmed replied. "I am extracting revenge for your part in the murder of my comrades twenty years ago. You do remember the incident, don't you?"

David Bin-Yishai thought about making a grab for Ahmed's pistol, but he knew he wouldn't succeed. His time had come, so he made a conscious decision not to give this man the satisfaction of seeing fear.

"How the hell do you expect me to remember?" Bin-Yishai said. "I have killed so many of you towelheads that it makes no more impact on me than stepping in a pile of camel shit."

The gun in Ahmed's hand made three whooshing sounds as the silencer deadened the sound of the shots.

Midnight,
Twenty-eight thousand feet over Missouri

John was cognizant of the whisper of the wind and engines outside the window of the United 767, but he was drifting comfortably in that half-sleep stage. Jenny was asleep as well, but Don Yee was working with his laptop computer, connected to the Internet via the seat-back phone in front of him. Tapping into the Los Angeles Police Department's computers, he began bringing up pictures of young females who had been arrested. One by one the girls' faces appeared on the screen before him. Some were mug shots, photographs taken when the subject had been arrested for such things as shoplifting, burglary, possession, prostitution, disturbing the peace, etc. Most of these pictures were of hard-looking women who were caught up in the system, angry and defiant. Occasionally, standing out like a rose among cabbages, there would be the sweet, freshly scrubbed face of a young girl more frightened than angry, more confused than defiant.

Don was going through the pictures rapidly, clicking them off and bringing them up one by one, until one of them caught his attention. The girl looking back from his screen had light brown hair, a slight smile, the suggestion of a dimple, and inquiring blue eyes set in a soft, pensive face. She was identified only as *"Tulip Smith, indigent female, age nineteen."*

"It's her," Don said quietly. He reached around the seat in front of him and touched John on the shoulder.

"Yes?" John said, rubbing his eyes and stretching. He looked through the window of the plane, but saw only blackness outside.

"I found her, John."

John was totally awake now.

"Where?"

"I found her on the LAPD file. She was picked

up just over three months ago for unauthorized occupancy."

"Good work, Don."

Hollywood Community Police Station

Ringing telephones, a dozen conversations, and a police scanner made the ready room of the Hollywood Station just short of pandemonium. John, Jenny, and Don, all wearing visitor's badges, stood beside Lieutenant Homer Jackson's desk as he tapped the keys on his computer.

"Here she is," he said. "She gave her name as Tulip Smith."

"And you let it go at that?" John asked. "You didn't bother to find out who she really was? Or even how old she was?"

"She gave her age as nineteen, and that was validated by her driver's license."

"She was seventeen."

The black police officer looked up at John and sighed. "Look, Mr. Barrone, this is Hollywood. Half the young women in the world come here hoping to be a movie star, and the other half wish they could come. Most of them are just naïve, overly ambitious kids. If they stray over the line, shoplift or deal in drugs, we'll be a little more aggressive in dealing with them. But in the case of Tulip Smith, the only thing we've ever picked her up on is unauthorized occupancy."

"Which is what exactly?" Jenny asked.

"She and some other girls were staying in an empty apartment building down on Logan and Sunset Boulevard."

"Who were the other girls?" John asked.

Lieutenant Jackson stroked his chin for a moment as he studied the three. "Now tell me again why you want this information," he said.

"I told you the girl is only seventeen. Tulip Smith, as you call her, is actually Annette Quinncannon. She ran away from home four months ago. Her grandfather has hired us to find her."

"Her grandfather?"

"Marist Quinncannon," Jenny said. "Perhaps you have heard of him?"

"Marist Quin—holy shit! *The* Marist Quinncannon?" Jackson asked. "The billionaire?"

"Give or take a million," John said.

"Damn, and I had his granddaughter right here in front of me. Wonder what it would've been worth to me if I had known who she was and called him then?"

"Trust me, Lieutenant, you don't want to know," John said. "It would just make you feel bad."

"Yeah, I guess so. Just a minute, let me check on something for you." Jackson picked up the phone and punched in a number. He waited a moment, then spoke again when the phone was answered. "Yeah, Larry, you want to come in here for a moment?" He put the phone down, then turned his attention back to John, Jenny, and Don.

"Sergeant Larry Wallace is in charge of Vice," he said. "He might be able to—wait a minute, here he is. I'll let him talk to you."

Sergeant Wallace was a large man, at least two inches taller and fifty pounds heavier than John. And though Wallace had a slight belly-rise, John had a feeling that much of his weight was muscle. He had gray eyes and a blotchy, reddish complexion. He wore his hair very short.

"What can I do for you, Lieutenant?"

"Bunny Miller," Jackson said. "Where is she working these days?"

"Damn, Lieutenant, you peddlin' poontang for her? Actually, I guess that would be coontang, wouldn't it? No offense meant, you being black and all."

It was clear by the expression on Jackson's face that he didn't find the joke humorous. "These people are looking for some information and I think she can provide it."

"What kind of information are you looking for?" Wallace asked.

"We are trying to locate Annette Quinncannon," John said. He showed Wallace a picture. "Do you know her?"

Wallace shook his head. "I've never seen her."

"Sure you have," Jackson said. "We had her in here once for unauthorized occupancy."

"Well, that means I *have* seen her," Wallace said. "But in my position I see a parade of these girls, and after a while they all start looking alike to me. For the life of me, though, I can't place her. What do you want with her?"

"Her family has hired us to find her," John said.

Wallace chuckled. "Good luck on that," he said. "It's been my experience that when these girls want to stay lost, they can do a pretty good job of it."

"I suggested that Bunny Miller might be able to help them," Jackson said.

"Sort of 'set a whore to find a whore,' is that it?" Wallace asked.

"Whore?" Jenny asked. "I thought you said you don't know this girl. If you don't know her, what makes you think she is a whore?"

"Because they are all whores," Wallace replied easily. "Look, most of these girls are on the street by their own choice. If their families had any sense, they would just forget them."

"Annette's family doesn't feel that way."

"Annette?"

"The girl's real name is Annette Quinncannon," Jackson said to Wallace. "And get this. She is Marist Quinncannon's granddaughter."

"Marist Quinncannon? Now, there's a man with a lot of money. You wouldn't think a girl would run away from that," Wallace said.

"It happens, even among the rich," John said.

"Yeah, I guess so, just like being a rich man's granddaughter doesn't mean she's not a whore," Wallace said.

"She has no record, does she?" John asked. "Has she ever been picked up for prostitution?"

"The lack of a record isn't as telling as the company she keeps," Wallace said. "She is obviously a friend of Bunny Miller, and Bunny has three arrests for prostitution."

"I must admit, Mr. Barrone, Sergeant Wallace has a point there," Jackson said. "These people do have a rather close-knit community."

"Do you think this person, Bunny, could help us find her?" Jenny asked.

"If she knows why you are looking for her, she will," said Jackson. "Bunny has a good head on her shoulders."

"A good head on her shoulders," Wallace scoffed. "She's a hooker, Lieutenant, pure and simple. I know she's a young, good-looking light-skinned black girl and that probably turns you on. But don't go giving her credit for things like having a heart of gold, or a good head on her shoulders, or anything like that. She's a whore, pure and simple."

"Do you know where she can be found?" John asked.

"Yeah, I think so," Wallace answered. "They say she's been working over on Aurel."

"Tell me about Bunny Miller, Lieutenant Jackson. Was she arrested with Annette?"

Jackson shook his head. "No, she wasn't arrested with her. She's the one who bailed Annette out."

SIX

"That's her," Don said, pointing to a young black woman standing in front of a liquor store. The woman was wearing a red leather thong, the back strap of which had totally disappeared in the crack of her ass.

"Oh, that has to be uncomfortable," Jenny said.

"Good advertising, though," Don Yee said.

John pulled up to the curb, and the young woman smiled as she walked out to the car. When she saw two men and a woman in the car, the smile was replaced by a look of confusion. She started to turn away.

"Wait!" John called. "Are you Bunny?"

"Are you cops?"

"No."

Bunny paused for a moment. "You know what happens if I ask you if you're cops and you say no, but turns out you are? That's entrapment, and they'll throw any case you try to make out of court."

"We're not cops," John said again. "You are Bunny, aren't you?"

"That's my name, honey."

"Good. Would you mind coming with us?"

"Come with you where?"

"Not far. We have a motel room near here."

"Say what? You want me to come with all three of you?"

"Don't worry, we'll pay you."

"Yeah, well, with three of you, it's goin' to cost three times what I normally get."

"Fine," John said.

Bunny smiled broadly. "Kinky," she said as she opened the door and slid into the backseat with Don Yee. She reached up to put her fingers on his cheek. "But that's okay, honey. I'm into kink."

"I've got olives, peppers, sausage, and I've got mushrooms and hamburger," Jenny said. "Who wants what?"

"I like everything but anchovies," Bunny said. "Honey, don't try to give me no pizza with anchovies. Ooh, those are nasty things."

"How about one slice of each?" Jenny offered, putting two wedge-shaped slices of pizza on a paper plate and carrying it over to Bunny, who was sitting on the edge of the bed.

"Thanks," Bunny said. She looked over at Don, who had one large pizza all by himself. "He really going to eat all that?" she asked.

"Plus what we don't eat," Jenny replied.

"He eat like that, how come he so skinny?"

"It's my genes," Don said.

"Lord, honey, if you could bottle those genes and sell them, you got 'ny idea how much money you would make?" Bunny asked.

Bunny had wrapped herself in a large bathroom towel to restore some modesty, if not dignity, to her near-nudity. She was sitting on the edge of the bed, looking at pictures on Don's laptop. She started to take a bite of pizza, then pulled the slice back down. "This is him," she said. "This is Uncle Billy. He's the last person I saw Tulip talkin' to. And I haven't seen her since that night."

"Did Tulip go with him?" Jenny asked.

Bunny shook her head. "No. Uncle Billy, he's really strange. He said she wasn't young enough, so he drove off. When I left, Tulip was still standin' out there on the corner."

"Is there a chance he may have come back for her?"

"There's a chance, I guess," Bunny said. "But if he did, I didn't see it."

"Then we haven't really accomplished anything," Jenny said with a disgruntled sigh.

"Maybe yes and maybe no," John said. "I think our next step is to talk to this man." John looked at the picture of Uncle Billy that Bunny had picked out. A few key-taps brought up information on the computer screen. "His name is Marvin Fry."

"Look, Uncle Billy is a strange man," Bunny said. "But if there's something bad happen to Tulip, I'd be willin' to bet anything that he didn't have nothin' to do with it. Besides, like I said, he drove off before I even left."

"But you said he could've come back," John said.

"Yes, but even if he did come back, I still don't think he's the kind that would hurt anyone."

"Try telling that to the Allendale School Board," Don said.

"What do you mean?"

"This man Fry, or Uncle Billy as you call him, was principal of the Allendale Middle School. He was fired for molesting seven young girls, none of whom was over twelve."

"Well, yes, it's no secret he likes young girls," Bunny said. "But all he did was molest them. I mean, he didn't hurt them, did he?"

"I doubt it's a memory any of them wants to hang on to," John said sardonically.

"Yeah, well, losing your cherry when you're eleven years old ain't like gettin' killed, you know what I mean? That's 'bout how old I was when I lost mine to my mother's boyfriend. And look at me. I didn't get hurt none by it."

Jenny looked at Bunny, but said nothing.

"I know what you thinkin'," Bunny said defensively. "But you don't know nothin' 'bout me. So, don't you be makin' no judgments on me, you hear? I do this 'cause I like it."

Defiantly, Bunny threw off her towel. "Folks do what they got a talent to do," she said. "And believe me, I got the talent."

"I'm, uh, sure you do," Jenny said.

After Bunny's outburst, they ate their pizza in silence. Then, when they were finished, John stood up. "You can stay here as long as you want," he said to Bunny.

"You going to look for Uncle Billy?"

"Yes."

"He likes to cruise Sunset Boulevard. He drives a big Lincoln Town Car. Dark blue, I think."

"Thanks."

"Listen," Bunny said as the three started to leave. "I hope you find Tulip. I've been wondering what happened to her. She was my friend, and I never did think she would just wander off like that."

"If you were her friend, why didn't you report her missing?"

"You think that would've done any good? Tulip

was a whore. The police don't care what happens to whores."

"We care," Jenny said softly. "If you hear anything, will you let us know?"

"How'm I goin' do that?"

Jenny wrote a number on a piece of paper. "This is my cell-phone number. You can call anytime, day or night."

It was past eleven that night when they saw the Lincoln cruising slowly down Sunset Boulevard.

"You have that red light?" John asked.

"Right here," Jenny answered, picking the light up from the floorboard.

"Where'd you get a red light?" Don asked from the backseat. "We don't have any authority to use a red light."

"We know that," John said. "But our friend in the Lincoln doesn't know it."

Plugging one end into the lighter socket, Jenny sat the light on top of the car. It was flashing as they came up beside the Lincoln. The driver of the Lincoln looked toward them, his eyes wide in fear and surprise.

"It's him," Jenny said.

"Motion for him to pull over."

Jenny did so, but the driver refused, accelerating instead.

"Damn!" John said, as the Lincoln suddenly shot ahead of them.

John pushed down on the accelerator, then pulled in behind him. Both cars gained speed quickly, and although the traffic wasn't heavy at this time of night, they were going much faster than was prudent. John was making no effort to pass him, but was staying glued to his tail.

"Pass him," Don Yee shouted excitedly.

"No need for that," John answered.

"If I were driving, I would pass him," Don said.

"If you were driving, we'd be wrecked by now," Jenny said. Don Yee was notorious for bad driving.

Ahead of them, the Lincoln pushed a red light and John went through right on his tail. The other cars in the intersection honked angrily and braked quickly, barely avoiding collision.

The Lincoln couldn't push the next red light, because it had changed too far before he got to the intersection. Out of the corner of his eye, John saw a tractor-trailer unit starting through, and he put on his brakes. He saw the taillights come on in front of him as the Lincoln driver also braked, but the Lincoln wasn't going to get stopped in time. The driver whipped the wheel to the left, and the car went into a sideways skid, sliding across the intersection. The truck honked and swerved, but couldn't entirely avoid the collision. It hit the Lincoln just on the corner of the right rear bumper, throwing it into a 360-degree spin. The Lincoln finally came to a rest, its backside smashed against a light pole on the street corner. The engine stalled and the driver was trying to restart the car when John pulled right up to him, bumper to bumper, making it impossible for the Lincoln to leave, even if the driver could get it started. Jenny and Don jumped out of the car and ran up to the Lincoln.

"Get out of the car, Uncle Billy!" Jenny called.

Uncle Billy got out and, without being asked, put both hands on the top of his car. Don Yee frisked him.

"I don't have a gun," Uncle Billy whined. "I don't carry a weapon."

"No, I don't suppose you really need a weapon with young girls," John said.

"I-I haven't done anything wrong," Uncle Billy said. "You don't have any right to arrest me."

"We're not arresting you," John said.

Uncle Billy looked surprised. "You're not?"

"No, we just want to ask you some questions. Would you come with us, please?"

"What if I don't want to go with you?"

"If you come with us voluntarily, then there won't be anything else to add to your record. Otherwise, we will arrest you," John said. He was running a bluff. They had no more authority to arrest Marvin Fry than they did to use the red light to run him down.

"I-I can't have anything else on my record. I'll go to jail if I do," Uncle Billy said. "All right, I'll come with you. What about my car?"

"Officer Barnes will drive your car," John said. He pointed to the rental car they were driving. "Get in."

By prior arrangement, Marist Quinncannon had made an office available to the Code Name Team in a building he owned on Santa Monica Boulevard. The office came completely furnished, including secretaries. The secretaries had been told only that John, Jenny, and Don were doing some investigative work for Mr. Quinncannon and that they were to do anything that was asked of them.

"What is this place?" Uncle Billy asked as they pulled into the parking garage of the building. "This isn't a police station."

"Is that really where you want to go? I thought you wanted to avoid the police station and the police blotter. I'm sure you realize that the police blotter is published every day. But of course, we can go the station if that's what you prefer," John said. Again he was running a bluff.

"No, no, this is fine," Uncle Billy said.

Jenny parked the damaged Lincoln alongside the rental car. Then she joined the others for the elevator ride up to the thirty-fifth floor. John nodded at the secretary as they passed through the reception area. He made no effort to introduce Uncle Billy to the secretary, and she was discreet enough not to ask any questions.

The office they led Uncle Billy into was plush. Floor-to-ceiling tinted windows afforded a magnificent view of the city. Recessed lighting made a soft show of the paintings and sculpture with which the office was decorated. A large, very expensive desk sat on a deep pile carpet.

Uncle Billy looked around the office, obviously impressed by its opulence. "What is this?" he asked. "I've never seen a police office like this."

"Our Uncle Billy is pretty smart, isn't he?" John said to Jenny and Don.

"My real name is Fry. Marvin Fry. I'd rather you call me that."

"Uncle Billy figured us out right away," Don said pointedly, ignoring Uncle Billy's request to be called Fry.

"Well, not right away. The red light had him believing we really were police officers," Jenny said.

"Wait a minute, hold on here," Uncle Billy said. "Are you telling me now that you aren't police?"

Smiling, John nodded his head. "We don't even like the police."

"If you aren't the police, who are you?"

"Like I told you, we are people who want to ask you some questions," John said.

"You want to ask me a few questions, but you aren't even with the police?" Uncle Billy shook his head. "Uh-uh, I don't have to answer a damned thing," he said defiantly. "I know my rights."

"He knows his rights," John said, chuckling.

"That's funny," Don added.

"What's funny about it?" Uncle Billy asked.

"You said it yourself, Uncle Billy," Jenny said. "We aren't policemen. That means, as far as we are concerned, you have no rights."

"I'm leaving here," Uncle Billy said, starting toward the door.

"No, I don't think you are," John said. "I think you'll talk to us."

"I'd like to see you make me talk," Uncle Billy said.

John nodded at Don, who put his hand at the junction of Uncle Billy's neck and shoulder, then applied pressure between his thumb and forefinger. Uncle Billy crumpled in pain.

"Sit down, Uncle Billy," John said quietly. "And we'll make this as quick and as painless as we can."

Holding his neck and shoulder, Uncle Billy sat in the nearest chair. "What is it?" he asked. "What do you want from me?"

"Have you ever seen this girl?" John asked, showing him a picture of Annette.

"No," Uncle Billy said quickly.

"Wrong answer," John said. He nodded at Don, who once again found a point where a slight application of pressure could create pain.

"Ouch! Stop! Don't!" Uncle Billy said. "Why are you doing that to me?"

"Now, I'm going to ask you again. Have you ever seen this girl?"

"I've never been with her," Uncle Billy said.

Don started to reach for him a third time, but Uncle Billy cringed and put up his hands. "Wait! I said I've never been with her. I didn't say I've never seen her."

John nodded and Don pulled away. "All right, Uncle Billy, that's a start," John said. "Where have you seen her?"

"She works on Sunset," he said. "That is, she used to. I haven't seen her in a long time."

"Tell us about the last time you saw her."

"I-I can't remember."

"You are trying my patience, Uncle Billy."

"Please, I told you, my name is Fry. Marvin Fry."

"That isn't what we heard. We heard you like the girls to call you Uncle Billy. The very young girls, that is."

"Listen, I've been straight ever since that little misunderstanding with the school board. The only girls I'm ever with now are working girls," Uncle Billy said quickly. "I didn't send them out onto the street, they are already there. Some of them are young, probably not as young as they tell me they are, but they are young. It's just a . . ." He let the sentence hang.

"It's just a what?"

"A game," Uncle Billy said. "It's just a game the girls and I play. I know they aren't really as young as they tell me." He nodded toward the picture. "As it turns out, Tulip might even be younger than she told me. At least, that's what I heard. But she didn't know how to play the game."

"Ah, so you were with her?" John asked.

"No, I talked to her, that's all. But like I say, she didn't know how to play the game."

"What does that mean?"

"When I asked her how old she was, she said she was nineteen. She should've said she was fifteen. That would've made it real good. I mean, I know she wasn't really that young, but if she had lied to me, it would've made things better. Later that same night, I got to thinking about her, so I came back. But I was too late. By the time I got back to her, I saw her getting into someone else's car."

"Can you describe the car?"

Uncle Billy shook his head. "I'm not sure. It might have been a Lexus or Mercedes, something like that. It looked expensive and foreign."

John sighed, then walked over to stand and look out the window. For a moment, he watched the aircraft approaching and departing from Los Angeles International Airport.

"John?" Don asked. "What are we going to do with him?"

"Let him go," John said.

"Thank you, thank you," Uncle Billy said, standing up quickly. "Oh, my car?"

"Here are your keys," Jenny said, tossing them to him.

"What about the damage?"

"I'd have that repaired if I were you," John said without turning away from the window. He made no offer of compensation for the damage to the car. Uncle Billy paused for a moment, as if he were about to suggest that perhaps someone might be responsible for the damage. Instead, he sighed, then nodded.

"Yes," he said. "I'd better have it repaired."

SEVEN

The Code Name Team was told they could live in the executive suite, an apartment of six thousand square feet and four bedrooms located on top of the Quinncannon Building. They chose instead to stay in the Sunset Motel, a non-franchise motel in a more modest part of town. Taking three adjoining rooms, they felt this location would be easier to work from than the plush penthouse.

During the week following their discussions with sunny and Uncle Billy, the three Code Team operatives were able to work out of the motel without arousing too much attention. They continued their search for Annette. For the most part, Don stayed in his room at the motel, confining his search to the Internet, tapping into every Jane Doe victim on the West Coast. In the meantime, John interviewed over a hundred street cops to see if any of them could provide any leads.

Jenny had her own way of looking.

"You go, girl, you lookin' good now," Bunny said as she backed away to examine her work. Jenny was in Bunny's apartment, having come to her for help in passing herself off as a hooker.

"I can't believe men really like this," Jenny said, examining the exaggerated makeup on her face.

"Honey, what you talkin' about? Whores been puttin' this shit on their face for a thousand years," Bunny said. "So there must be some reason for it. Men don't like their wives or girlfriends or sisters to look like this. But you try and work the street without it and see how far you get."

"You may have a point," Jenny said.

"Now, we got to get you the right kind of clothes." Bunny opened the door to her closet, looked through it for a moment, then took something out and tossed it on the bed. "Put this on."

Jenny looked at the ounce or so of cloth, then screwed her face up into a frown. "Put it on what? My left tit? That's about all that dress would cover. I can't wear that."

Bunny laughed. "Why you so shy, girl? You got a good body for someone your age."

"Someone my age?" Jenny replied sharply. "What do you mean, someone my age?"

Bunny laughed again. "Well don't have a shit-fit over it. I was givin' you a compliment, is all."

"Compliments like that I don't need," Jenny said. She sighed, then picked up the dress Bunny had selected for her. "All right, let's do it."

One hour later both women were out on Sunset Boulevard. There were several other girls out tonight as well, and Bunny approached three of them who were standing together near a strip joint.

"Bunny, what you doin' back here, girl?" one of the others asked. "I thought you moved your ass over to Beverly."

"I been working Aurel, but I thought I'd come back over here tonight where there's no competition 'cept you ladies, and you no competition at all," Bunny teased. The girls laughed.

"Woo, listen to that girl talk. Who's your friend?"

"She's new to the world," Bunny said. "I'm showin' her the ropes."

"Welcome to the street, girl," one of them said. "You just divorced, huh?"

"Beg your pardon?"

"When someone don't start to whorin' till they're your age, more'n likely they're just divorced."

"Oh, yes, that is what happened to me. I'm just divorced."

"Yeah, that happened to a friend of mine. She divorced her husband, then not one month later she saw his sorry ass down here lookin' to pick up a woman. Girl, don't you know she went home with him and charged him for what she'd been givin' him for free."

"You lyin'," one of the others said.

"Gospel truth," the first said, holding up her hand as all, including Jenny, laughed. She turned to Jenny. "So, what's your name, girl?"

Jenny hesitated for a moment, then said the first name that popped into her head. "Linda."

The girl shook her head. "No, that won't do."

"I beg your pardon?"

"You got to have yourself some kind of classy name if you workin' the street. Linda, hell, that could be anybody. Half the johns out there have wives named Linda, and the other half have sisters. They sure don't want to be payin' money to screw a Linda."

Again, the girls laughed.

"Now, you take me. My real name is Norma Jean. I'm just little old Norma Jean Collier from Blodgett, Missouri. But out here I am Sheeba. You know, as in Queen Sheeba?"

"Actually she wasn't Queen Sheeba, she was Queen *of* Sheeba," Jenny said.

"The hell you say. Well, I kind of like the name Sheeba anyway. Now, we have to get you a name."

"How about René?" one of the other girls asked.

"Yes," Sheeba said. "René. Now, there's a classy name for you." She smiled at Jenny. "Girl, from now on, you are René."

For the first few days, Jenny managed to avoid having to face the issue of actually going with someone. She did this by being considerably less aggressive than the other girls. She watched as they worked their johns, and even managed a reluctant admiration of the skill with which they plied their avocation.

But Jenny did more than watch; she also questioned, pushing her investigation to the point that some of the girls became uncomfortable with all the questions and began shying away from her.

On the fourth day, as always, she had hung back during the early hours when the johns were most plentiful and the girls most aggressive. Now she was one of the very few left as she saw a purple Cadillac with a gold Rolls-Royce grille stop at the curb. Three men got out of the car. The driver was a small black man, dressed in a yellow three-piece suit and a wide-brimmed Panama hat. Several chains of gold hung around his neck, and he had gold earrings and a gold nose ring.

The other two men were huge and muscular, one white and one black. All three went toward Sheeba, who, upon seeing them, started to walk away.

"Don't you be runnin' from me, bitch!" the small driver called to her.

"Now, Uptown, you've got no call to be coming after me," Sheeba said in a frightened voice. "I haven't been holding out on you."

"You either holdin' out or you ain't puttin' out," Uptown said. "I think maybe an ass-whippin' will show you I mean business."

"No!" Sheeba said, holding her arms up protectively. "Don't hit me. Please, don't hit me."

"Leave her alone," Jenny called.

Until that moment, Uptown and his two goons had been concentrating so on Sheeba that they hadn't even noticed Jenny. When she called out to them, Uptown stopped as abruptly as if he had been slapped. He turned toward Jenny.

"Say what?" he asked, as if he couldn't believe his ears.

"I said leave her alone," Jenny repeated.

"Well, I'll just be damned. I thought that's what you said. Maybe I'd better introduce myself. My name is Uptown Morris and Sheeba is one of my girls."

"I don't care who you are. I'm not going to stand by and let you hurt her."

"What's that? You ain't goin' *let* me hurt her?" Uptown asked. He put his hands on his hips, cocked his head, and looked at the two large goons with him. "Did I hear right? Did she just say she ain' goin' *let* me hurt one o' my own bitches?"

"That's what she said," the white goon replied.

"Well, I be damn, I thought that what she said." Uptown turned back toward Sheeba. "You just wait right here for me. Soon's I take care of this bitch, I be comin' back for you."

"Run, René!" Sheeba shouted.

Jenny stood her ground while Uptown and the two bigger men walked toward her.

"Run!" Sheeba shouted again.

"You better listen to the bitch," the little man in the yellow suit said. He smiled broadly, evilly, showing a gold tooth.

"Why should I run from you?"

"Because I'm Uptown Morris, and I bring the fear of God into the girls who work my turf."

"I've never heard of you."

Uptown looked surprised. "Girl, I can't believe you so dumb you've never heard of me. You ask any girl on the street who is Uptown Morris, and they'll tell you. 'Uptown Morris,' they say, 'is my main man. He's the one look out for me.' What about you, girl? You got someone to look out for you?"

"No."

"Well, then, you in luck, ain't you? 'Cause after I give your ass a beatin' for buttin' into somethin' that ain't none of your business, I'm goin' to let you sign up with me. You do want to sign up with Uptown Morris, don't you?"

"Why would I want to do that?"

"Just how dumb are you? How long you been peddlin' your ass?"

"She's new, Uptown," Sheeba said. "Please don't hurt her. She doesn't understand."

"It's time she learned," Uptown said. "Here's how it works, girl. When you out here peddlin' your ass, you workin' on my turf, and anyone workin' on my turf has to pay for the privilege. I get seventy percent."

"Seventy percent? You're charging seventy percent and there are actually girls who will pay this?"

"All of them pay it."

"That's preposterous," Jenny said. Although she had no intention of ever earning a cent as a prostitute, she couldn't imagine anyone who did paying this odd little man seventy percent of what they earned. "I won't do it," she said.

"I'm real sorry you feel that way," Uptown said. "But maybe after my two associates talk to you, you'll change your mind." Uptown stepped to one side, then nodded slightly toward the two who were with him. He smiled as they started toward Jenny.

Jenny moved, almost imperceptibly, to the balls of her feet. The goons were big and there were two of them. If she were to have any chance at all of escaping serious injury at their hands, she would need every advantage she could muster, including surprise.

She let them come one step closer, then suddenly pivoted around on her left foot, sending her right foot hard into the groin of the big black man. At the same time she brought the knife-edge of her hand around in a whistling smash into the Adam's apple of the big white man.

Both thugs grunted in pain and grabbed their injured parts. That provided the opening Jenny needed, and she switched blows, this time crashing the knife-edge of her hand into the black man's Adam's apple, and the spike of her heel into the white man's groin. With both of the men doubled over in pain, she finished them off with a kick into the sides of their heads. They went down.

"What the hell?" Uptown shouted in alarm when he saw how easily and quickly she had taken care of his enforcers. His hand started inside his jacket, but Jenny took him by the wrist, jerked his arm down, and flipped him. As she did so, she reached up to grab the nose ring, jerking it out as she flipped.

Uptown let out a yelp of pain as blood began spurting from the wound. Now lying flat on his back, he put his hand to his nose, then, feeling the torn flesh, pulled it back and looked at the blood on the palm of his hand.

"You bitch!" Uptown shouted. "You're dead! You hear me, bitch! You are dead meat!"

Once more he reached inside his jacket pocket. When he couldn't come up with what he was looking for, his face registered an expression of surprised anger.

"Are you looking for this, little man?" Jenny asked, holding up the pistol that she had lifted from his holster when she flipped him.

"What the hell?" Uptown shouted. "How'd you get that?" He started to get up, but Jenny put the barrel of the pistol to his crotch.

"Hold it! Hold it! What you doin'?" Uptown turned his head to one side, then began quivering in fear.

"How would you like to be lead soprano singer for the New Supremes?" Jenny asked matter-of-factly. She pulled the hammer back.

"No, no, please!" Uptown said.

"Come to think of it, you probably have a terrible voice," Jenny said. She nodded toward the two musclemen, who were just now beginning to get themselves up. "Tell those two muscle-bound, brain-dead, limp-dick bastards to put their guns on the ground, then get back into that pimpmobile of yours," Jenny said.

"What about me? Can I go?" Uptown asked.

"You too," Jenny said, pulling the gun back to let Uptown get up. "But know this, asshole. If I ever see you or either of these two bastards again, I will shoot you on sight. Do you understand me, Mr. Uptown Morris?"

"Yeah, yeah, I understand," Uptown said. He

looked over at his two bodyguards, who were just now sitting up. "Put down your guns and get into the car, both of you," he shouted.

Groggily, the two men did as ordered. Then, holding a handkerchief to the bloody wound on his nose, Uptown slid behind the wheel. With a roar of his engine and a squeal of tires, he drove off.

As the car sped off down the street, Jenny heard Sheeba clapping behind her. "That was wonderful!" she said.

"Why was he after you?" Jenny asked.

"He thinks I'm holding back on him," Sheeba said.

"Well, for seventy percent, I'd be holding back on him too."

Sheeba shook her head. "You really are a virgin, aren't you? Where did you learn to do that?"

"Do what?"

"Fight like that," Sheeba said. "Every girl on the street is afraid of Uptown and his two goons, but you didn't have any trouble at all."

"It's because they weren't expecting it," Jenny said. "Believe me, it won't be that easy the next time."

"Maybe they won't come back."

"Don't kid yourself. They'll be back. His kind always do."

"You didn't just get divorced an' go into the life," Sheeba said. "You aren't really one of us at all, are you?"

Jenny didn't answer.

"Are you a cop, down here to bust us all?"

Jenny shook her head. "No. I'm not a cop. At least, not the way you think."

"Not in the way I think? So what does that mean?"

"I'm sort of a private investigator," Jenny said.

"And you are looking for Tulip?"

"Yes."

"I thought maybe you were, what with all the questions you were asking about her. She's a runaway, isn't she? Her family is trying to find her?"

"Yes. Tulip's real name is Annette Quinncannon."

"The thing Tulip's family doesn't understand is that she doesn't want to be found," Sheeba said.

"Why do you say that?"

"It's one thing to whore, you do that pretty much in private, and if you ever go back home, there's a chance no one will ever find out. But what if you decide to leave the life and marry some nice guy, then at some party someday someone puts in a videotape and there you are, big as life."

"A videotape?" Jenny felt a charge of excitement. This was the first real piece of information they had been able to pick up since their discussion with Uncle Billy.

"Yeah, you know, the X-rated videos?"

"Are you telling me Tulip is making porn movies?"

"Yes."

"How do you know?"

"I've seen her."

"You've seen her making the movies?"

"I've seen her *in* the movies. Or at least one of them. You see, a lot of the johns enjoy watching porn movies while we're having sex. I saw her in one of those."

"What was the name of the film, do you remember?"

Sheeba laughed. "You ever seen any of those movies? Who knows the names of them? All I know is I have definitely seen her."

EIGHT

The sign in front of the store read: "Welcome to Eros Entertainment, California's Largest Adult Video Store."

Inside, it looked like a large department store—clean and well lighted, with scores of display racks. It was also as crowded as any department store, with men and women, many of them well dressed and affluent-looking, moving up and down the aisles, examining the explicit pictures on the outside of thousands of video boxes.

Each aisle was identified by a sign that told the prospective customer what he or she might find there, such as: "Amateur Sex, Threesomes, S&M, Uncles, Lesbian, Gay," and several others.

"What the hell do you think 'Uncles' sex is?" John asked Don.

A female store employee overheard the question.

"It's a story in which a young girl is seduced by her uncle," the employee explained. She was dressed in a blue dress with a neck that was scooped so low that the tops of her breasts were exposed nearly to the nipples. In addition, the dress was so short that her panties could be seen under the hemline. She was carrying a shepherd's crook.

"You mean there is an entire genre of that sort of thing?" John asked.

"Oh, yes," the young woman replied. "We like to cater to all tastes." She smiled. "I'm Bo Peep. I'm in charge of the fairy-tale section. May I help you find something?"

"We are looking for a movie in which this girl may have acted," John said, showing Annette's picture. "Have you ever seen her?"

Bo Peep looked at the picture, then nodded. "Yes, I think so."

"What was she in?"

Bo Peep shook her head. "I'm not sure I remember. We have over ten thousand videos," she said. "I have seen maybe a thousand, but I haven't seen them all."

"Thanks."

"She looks pretty young, so you might try the Cheerleaders section," Bo Peep suggested. She pointed out the part of the store where that section could be found.

The Cheerleaders section was watched over by a young woman who was dressed in a very short, pleated skirt alternating in colors of red and black, with a red sweater and holding a black megaphone. She was carrying red and black pom-poms.

"Hello, I'm Bambi," the girl said. Her blond hair hung in pigtails, and her face was without makeup, giving her a freshly scrubbed, virginal look. Although John was certain she was older, she looked about fifteen, which, of course, was exactly the image she was trying to project.

"Bambi, we're looking for a movie in which this girl may have starred," John said, showing her the picture.

Bambi examined the picture for a moment, then

shook her head. "I don't recognize her right off-hand," she said. "But you are welcome to look at the film sleeves. Maybe you'll find her picture on the outside of one of them."

"Thanks," John said.

They didn't find her picture in Eros Entertainment, nor in any of the other adult video stores they looked through over the next few days. Then one evening, as the three were discussing their shrinking options, Jenny's cell phone rang.

"It's me, Bunny. You still trying to find that porn flick that Tulip is in?"

"Yes," Jenny said. "Do you have it?"

"No," Bunny said. "But I know where you can get it."

"Where?"

"Twenty-one Seventeen Industrial Circle," Bunny said. "Ten o'clock tonight."

Bunny was standing at a public telephone in the parking lot of a convenience store. She hung up the phone, then looked back at the big man who had brought her there. He was holding a gun on her.

"I did like you told me," Bunny said.

"Yes, and you did that very well too," the man said. "I give you an A."

"I don't want no A. What I want is for you to let me go."

The man shook his head. "Sorry, girlie, I can't do that."

"Why not? I did what you told me to do."

"Ah, but we have other plans for you," the man said.

"What sort of plans?" Bunny asked. "I don't

need nobody makin' any plans for me. What I do, I do for myself."

The man made a waving motion with his pistol. "Get in the car," he said.

Bunny shook her head. "No," she said. "I ain't goin' do that."

"Get in the car or I'll kill you right here, right now."

Bunny shook her head again. "No, you won't. You won't kill me right in the middle of town."

"The middle of town? Look around you, bitch," the man said. "This look like the tourist section of town to you? I could shoot you right now and you wouldn't be anything but one more dead nigger. Now which is it? Do you get in the car, or do I shoot you?"

"I'll get in the car," Bunny said.

"Good girl."

"What's going to happen to them? To those folks you had me call?"

"You don't worry about them," the man said. "You got your own problems."

Although the alley was liberally lined with street lamps, only about one out of every three were still burning. The yellow bars of light that spilled from those pale bulbs did little to push away the darkness. As John drove slowly up the alley, the car moved in and out of those little glowing pools so that they were passing from light into darkness and from darkness to light, again and again, in a flashing effect.

It was as if they had stumbled into a ghost town, or at least a ghost section of town. The buildings were all empty, with the windows and doors boarded over. The loading docks behind the buildings were in various states of disrepair, and trash containers were overflowing with refuse. A large sign indicated that the entire area was being razed to make room for the future home of a new sports stadium and convention center.

"Are you sure this is the place?" Jenny asked.

"Twenty-one Seventeen Industrial Circle. That's the address she gave, and that's where we are."

John stopped the car and they looked around. A rat darted out from the darkness behind a trash container and into a pool of light, where it pulled the last remnants of a hamburger bun from its wrapper. Then, with its beady eyes ever alert for danger, it bounded quickly back to the container with its prize.

"What a filthy, disgusting place," Jenny said. "Why would anyone even consider putting a video store back here?"

"Maybe the rent is cheap," Don suggested. "But what I'm wondering is, who are their customers?"

"You can be sure they're not walk-in trade," John replied. "If you want to know the truth, I think we're on a wild-goose chase, but we've come this far, so we may as well check it out."

John opened the door and when he did, the interior light came on. Almost instantly gunfire erupted, and tracers streamed out of the darkness, slamming into the car and smashing through the windows.

"Get down! Out of the car!" John shouted as he fell through the open door, then rolled away from the car. Don and Jenny followed suit. All the while guns continued to fire, and the air was filled with the angry pop and whine of deadly missiles.

From the far end of the alley there was a loud swooshing sound. A streak of flame, much larger than the illuminated tracer rounds, raced through the alley toward the car.

"Rocket launcher!" John shouted. He covered his head with his arms just when the rocket hit the car. The car erupted in a billowing rose of flame. His ears hurt from the concussion as the detonation sent shock waves rolling out from the point of impact. The hood and doors of the car flew up and out from the explosion, causing twisted pieces of flaming-hot metal to come raining back down.

The burning car lit up the dark alley, and John low-crawled to a rack of garbage cans. In the flickering light and dark shadows, he saw both Don and Jenny moving into positions of shelter and concealment. That assured him that they were still alive and that they had had the presence of mind to get out of sight.

"Son of a bitch! Did you see that?" a voice called from the other end of the alley.

"Quiet, you dumb shit!" a more authoritative voice replied. "Listen!"

"What are we listening for?" a third voice asked.

"Quiet!"

For a long moment nothing could be heard but the snapping flames of the burning car, and the distant clanging of a harbor bell.

"Ernie, check it out," the authoritative voice ordered.

"Screw you, Meeker! I'm not goin' down that alley by myself."

"Cleetus?"

"Me neither."

"All right, we'll all go together."

John let them start up the alley. He knew he wouldn't have to compromise his position to tell Jenny and Don what to do. They would know.

"Keep your eyes peeled," Meeker said.

"Peeled for what?" Ernie replied. "You ask me, they're dead meat."

John waited until they were fully committed into the alley. Then, when they had nowhere to go, he stood up.

"Hey, asshole, this is one piece of meat that isn't dead," he said in a loud but calm voice.

"He's over there!" Cleetus shouted.

Once again, the alley was filled with the sound of automatic-weapons fire.

"No, we're over here!" Jenny called.

The three assailants turned their weapons toward the sound of the new voice. Glowing tracer bullets sprayed out from the guns, whizzing through the alley and bouncing off the brick walls on either side.

By contrast, there were only a few quick bangs from John's, Jenny's, and Don's guns. But those few well-placed shots were all that was required, for all three thugs went down.

Crouching low, John raced up the dark alley to the three men. The first two he checked were dead. The third, the one who had been the leader of the group, was moaning softly.

"Who sent you, Meeker?" John asked.

Meeker didn't answer.

"That is your name, isn't it? Didn't I hear one of the others call you Meeker?"

"Screw you," the victim said, his voice weak and strained.

"What was all this about? Why did you ambush us?"

"For one hundred thousand dollars," Meeker said. He tried to laugh, but the laugh turned into spastic coughing.

"Who paid you?"

"I can't tell you that. It's a matter of professional ethics."

"What profession? What ethics?" John asked.

In the distance, they could hear the sound of police sirens. Meeker coughed again, then groaned in pain. "Listen to 'em. Only time I've ever wanted the cops and they ain't goin' to make it here in time to save my ass, are they?"

"I'm afraid not," John said bluntly. "You'll be dead by the time they get here."

"Ain't that a bitch, though?"

"Who hired you?" John asked again.

"Satan hired me," Meeker said. He laughed. "You know, when you stop to think about it, that's funny, isn't it? I mean, working for Satan."

"It's hilarious," John said. He began rifling through Meeker's pockets until he found a set of car keys. "I'm going to have to borrow your car."

"Yeah, well be careful with it, will you? I just had it washed," Meeker said. He laughed, but the laugh turned to painful, spastic coughing.

By now Don and Jenny had joined John.

"Has he told you anything?" Don asked.

"No," John said. He held up the keys. "But he has been generous enough to give us his car."

The police sirens grew more insistent.

"Sounds like they are getting closer. I think we'd better get out of here," Jenny suggested. Leaving the wheezing, dying Meeker behind, the three hurried through the dark until they found Meeker's Mercedes.

"Damn, would you look at this? We're in the

wrong business. These hit men drive nice cars," Jenny said. They drove away just moments before the police arrived on the scene.

"That bitch Bunny set us up," Jenny said.

"Maybe it wasn't her fault," John suggested.

"What do you mean, it wasn't her fault? She told us where to go—we went there and look what happened."

"I think we should give her the benefit of the doubt until we know for sure why she did it. Maybe she didn't have any choice. There is a good side to this, though," John said.

"And what would that be? The fact that we didn't get killed back there?" Don asked.

"Well, there is that," John said. "But also the fact that we must be getting close to something, or someone. That was no incidental shoot-out back there. They were professional assassins hired to hit us."

"Who hired them?" Jenny asked.

"Satan hired them."

"What?"

John shook his head. "That's something Meeker said. He told me they were hired by Satan."

"So, do you think he was trying to make a joke, or was he just engaging in metaphorical musing?" Don asked.

"Could be a little of both," John replied.

"I would still like to know who set us up."

"Well, as my Chinese ancestors would say, let's look at this logically," Don said.

"Chinese ancestors my ass," Jenny replied, laughing. "Your family has been in America longer than mine."

"That's true," Don agreed. "Legend has it that my honorable great-great-great-great-grandfather taught Thomas Jefferson how to use the abacus."

John laughed, then asked, "What is this logical approach you were talking about?"

"Whoever set us up has to come from a very short list of names," Don replied. "And that short list is composed of people we have encountered since beginning this operation."

"All right, let's list them," John said. "There is Bunny obviously."

"And Sheeba," Jenny added.

"Uncle Billy," Don suggested.

"That's all," Jenny said. "Nobody else knows what we are doing."

"What about that pimp you ran into? What was his name?"

"Uptown," Jenny replied. "Uptown Morris. But I don't think he's behind this."

"Why not?"

"As far as he knows, I'm just another whore. No, this has to be someone who is on to what we are trying to do, and so far, that is only Bunny, Sheeba, and Uncle Billy."

"So, where do we go from here?" Don asked.

"Let's go talk to Uncle Billy again," John suggested.

"He gives me the creeps. Why do we want to see him?" Jenny asked.

"I still think he is our best lead to Annette. Not only is he the last person we know who saw her alive, he is also a pedophile. And we all agree that if Annette is making porn movies, she's playing the role of a very young girl, right?"

"Right," Jenny agreed.

"When you want to talk about bread, you go to

a baker. When you want to talk about child pornography, you go to a pedophile, and while Uncle Billy isn't much, he's the only one we have."

"But we have looked at three or four hundred video sleeves with that kind of theme, cheerleading, Girl Scouts, even uncles." Jenny shivered. "Uncles as in Uncle Billy," she added.

"We've only looked in the legal places," Don said. "I wouldn't be surprised to find an entire subrosa industry dealing in illegal porn."

"In today's society, what in the world is illegal now?" Jenny asked.

"Any sex scene involving anyone under the age of eighteen," Don said. "Illegal, but as long as there is a lucrative market for them, such films will be made."

"Which brings us right back to Uncle Billy," John said.

"Lead on, MacDuff," Jenny said.

They decided to wait until the next morning to see Uncle Billy. He lived in an upper-middle-class neighborhood. The street was tree-shaded; the houses were mostly large, mostly brick, and set deep in well-tended lawns of putting-green grass. It was the kind of neighborhood that an advertiser would choose to represent America; latest-model cars in the two- and three-car garages, riding lawn mowers, outdoor pools, lawn furniture, decorative lighting, and signs indicating that the community had a neighborhood watch.

Parking on the street in front, John, Jenny, and Don walked up the long sidewalk through the whispering whish of lawn sprinklers. The little droplets of water hanging in the grass flashed in all the colors of the rainbow.

There was a little business card in a holder under the doorbell button. The card read, "Marvin Fry, Ph.D."

"Damn," Don said. "This guy has his doctorate."

"He was a school principal," John said.

"He still gives me the creeps," Jenny added.

The smile on Uncle Billy's face faded immediately when he saw who had rung his doorbell.

"What do you want?" he asked.

"We want to talk to you," John said.

"I don't want to talk to *you*."

"You misunderstood what I said. I didn't say you wanted to talk to *us*, I said we wanted to talk to *you*." John pushed his way in.

"Hey, you can't do that!" Uncle Billy said. "Not unless you have a warrant."

John chuckled. "I thought we went through that with you already. We aren't policemen, Uncle Billy. Therefore we can do anything we want."

"Don't call me Uncle Billy."

"Would you rather we call you perverted asshole?" Jenny asked.

Uncle Billy looked over at Jenny and sighed. "I don't expect someone like you to understand someone like me. I'm not the monster you think I am."

"As far as I'm concerned, anyone who screws little girls is a monster," Jenny said.

"I've never forced myself on anyone."

"Jesus, and that's supposed to make it all right?"

"What do you want? I don't like people who look like you coming to my house," Uncle Billy said.

"People who look like us? And how do we look?" John asked.

"You look like plainclothes policemen. I'm afraid my neighbors might jump to the wrong conclusions."

"They probably think you are a low-life creep," Jenny said. "How is that conclusion wrong?"

"Please, go away. I'll meet you somewhere else."

"I tell you what, Uncle Billy. You help us out, and we'll be out of here as quickly as we can," John said.

"What do you want?"

"Did you set us up last night?" Jenny asked.

"What?"

"Did you arrange to have us killed?"

"No!" Uncle Billy said with a gasp. "How could you even think such a thing? Why would you even ask that question?"

"We were given a lead last night," John said. "When we followed up on the lead, we were ambushed. Three men tried to kill us."

"Well, it wasn't me," Uncle Billy said. "I would never do anything like that."

"You know what? I believe you," Jenny said.

"You believe me?"

"Yes. When you get right down to it, I don't think you have the balls to do something like that."

"Is that it? Is that all you wanted?"

"No," John replied. "I want to ask you about kiddie porn. You know, X-rated movies with very young girls?"

"How young?"

"Oh, let's say, under eighteen, young."

"Films like that are illegal," Uncle Billy said.

"Where can I buy films like that?"

"It's not only against the law to sell them, it's against the law to even own one," Uncle Billy added nervously.

"Yes, I'm sure it is," John said. "But if you remember, we aren't the law. So I don't really give a rat's ass what is legal and what isn't. My only concern is in finding Annette Quinncannon, by whatever means necessary. Now, answer my question. If I wanted some kiddie porn, where would I go?"

Uncle Billy was quiet for a long moment.

"You do want us out of your life, don't you, Uncle Billy?" John prodded.

"Yes, more than you can possibly imagine, I want you out of my life."

"Then help us out. The quicker we complete our job, the quicker we'll be out of here."

Uncle Billy sighed. "Go to www dot chickenhawk, underscore LA, dot com."

"What?" John asked, confused.

"He just gave us a Web address," Don said. "Where is your computer?" he asked.

"In here," Uncle Billy said.

John, Jenny, and Don followed Uncle Billy through the front of the house to a small room in the back. This room was set up as an office. There were several documents and plaques on the wall, including one for "Educator of the Year." There were several books around the computer.

"Excuse the mess," Uncle Billy apologized. "I, uh, can't work in the public school system anymore, and none of the private schools will hire me, so I'm making my living by writing textbooks." He moved some of the mess out of the way so Don could get to the computer keyboard.

Don signed onto the Internet, then went to *chickenhawk_la.com*. The Web site page was blank except for a drawing of a chicken hawk and a message that said, "Provide e-mail address."

Don put in an e-mail address, then clicked send.

A few minutes later he got a notice for mail. When he opened the letter he saw nothing but an address.

"What is this address?" John asked Uncle Billy.

"That's probably a street intersection," Uncle Billy said. "It usually is. If you are standing there on that corner, a van will stop. If you give the correct signal, the side door will slide open. Then you get into the van and ride around with them while you are making your video selection."

"Sounds complicated," Jenny said.

"It's meant to be complicated," Uncle Billy replied.

"Will they pick up anyone?" John asked.

"Anyone who gives the correct signal."

"What is the signal?"

"What is tomorrow? The date?" Uncle Billy asked.

"The seventh," Jenny replied.

Uncle Billy walked over to a marble fireplace mantel. Touching a button just inside the fireplace released an electronic lock, causing one of the marble panels to pop open slightly. Uncle Billy opened it the rest of the way, then took out five kiddie porn films and one computer-generated document.

"If you want to, you can look through these for the girl you are looking for," he said. "But I don't think you will find her." He opened the computer-generated document, then ran his finger down several lines. "If tomorrow is the seventh, the secret sign will be to hold your wrists crossed in front of you, with the forefinger and little finger of the left hand extended."

"Damn, a daily code book," John said. "That's a pretty sophisticated operation."

"Their names are Doc and Kate."

"Doc and Kate? That's all?"

"We don't socialize," Uncle Billy said. "That's all I know. By the way, I'd advise only one of you to go."

Don Yee was standing at the corner indicated by the e-mail address when, at exactly two P.M., a blue Ford van stopped. The driver glanced toward Don, and Don gave the appropriate signal. Almost instantly the side door opened.

"Get in, quickly," a woman's voice said from inside.

Don stepped into the van, the door closed behind him, and the van drove away.

There were only two people in the van, the driver and the woman who had told him to get in.

"I've never seen you before," the woman said. She was a thin woman with gray hair and dry, very wrinkled skin. Because of the condition of her skin, it was difficult to tell how old she was, but Don decided she must be in her late fifties to early sixties.

"No, but I was told I could join the network," Don replied, saying the words Uncle Billy had told him.

The woman looked at Don for a long moment, as if studying him.

"What do you think, Kate?" the driver called back over his shoulder.

"He looks all right to me, Doc," the woman answered.

"Thanks," Don said.

"Here's the way it works," Kate explained. "We will drive in the direction we are now going for three minutes; then we will turn around and come back.

You must have the transaction completed by that time."

"Where are the videos?" Don asked.

"In here." Kate opened a felt-lined panel on the side of the van. Behind the panel was a rack of one hundred pockets. Each pocket was filled with a video.

"Wait a minute," Don said as he looked at the rack. "There are no pictures."

"You want pictures, you have to pay for them," Kate said. She opened a briefcase and took out a stack of pictures, culled from the sleeve art. Each picture was coded, by number, to the corresponding video. Don reached for the pictures.

"Not so fast," Kate said, pulling the stack away. "It will cost you fifty dollars to look."

"Fifty dollars, just to look at the pictures to decide which film I want?" Don replied indignantly.

"This is to discourage the curious. Each video is one hundred dollars," the woman said. "If you buy one, you will get credit for the fifty dollars."

"Oh, well, that's more like it," Don said, handing her a fifty-dollar bill.

Don began looking through the pictures. The van reached the end of its three-minute drive, then turned around.

"You'd better hurry, mister," the woman said. "You have three minutes left, and you don't get a second chance."

"I haven't found what I'm looking for," Don said.

"Tell me what you want. Maybe I can help."

Don showed the woman the picture of Annette, and she studied it for a moment, then nodded.

"Yes, I know that one. I think I've got one of her left," she said. She rifled through the stack of pictures, then selected one and handed it to Don. "Would this be her?"

"Yes," Don said.

The woman nodded. "Three months ago, you could've bought this tape in any store. But it turned out she was underage, so they pulled all the tapes off the market. That's when we got them." She pointed to the picture. "This girl is probably legal by now."

"Yeah, that's just the age I like," Don said. "I want them young, but not so young they don't even have tits."

The woman snorted. "You don't have to worry about that, you aren't going to find any that young in here. You say you want this one?"

"Yes."

"That'll be fifty more dollars."

The van stopped.

"Take it or leave it before the light turns," the woman ordered.

"I'll take it," Don said, handing her another fifty. She gave him the video, then opened the door. Don stepped out onto the street, the door slid shut behind him, and the van drove off.

Bunny had no idea where she was, or how long she had been there. She was handcuffed to a steel bunk bed in a way that would allow her to lie down or sit on the edge of the bed.

The room was small and dirty. Through a small window on the back wall, she could hear automobile traffic, but because she couldn't walk around, she wasn't able to look through it. The traffic sounded far off to her, as if it were on the other side of a big field.

When she was brought there last night, she'd started screaming, hoping someone would hear her. She'd screamed until her throat was raw and she couldn't make another sound, but nobody had come. She'd finally fallen asleep from sheer exhaustion, waking up after daylight.

Now the daylight was fading, tone and tint. She had been right here, handcuffed to this bed, for the entire day. No one had come to offer her food, or water, or the opportunity to go to the bathroom. She was beginning to wonder if they were just going to let her stay here until she died.

She was asleep when, finally, someone came. When she opened her eyes, she saw that it was dark again.

"Let me go," Bunny said. "Please, let me go."

"I'm sorry, girlie, I can't do that," a gruff voice said. The man grabbed her by her upper arm.

"What are you doing?" Bunny asked.

"This will make you feel better," the man said, holding up a needle and syringe.

"Uh-uh," Bunny said, shaking her head. "I don't do no drugs. Maybe a little pot, but no drugs." She felt a sting in her arm. "What you do, man? I tol' you, I don't do no drugs."

"You'll feel better in a little while," the man said.

Bunny tried hard to look at the man's face, but it began to slip out of focus. She felt herself becoming dizzy; then her head felt heavy, so heavy she could barely hold it up. "What—was—that?" she asked. To her, the words sounded slow and drawn out, like a recording played at the wrong speed. She slipped into unconsciousness.

When Bunny came to, she was bound to what appeared to be a stone wall, held by shackles at her hands and feet. She didn't know where she was, or even how she had gotten there. The last thing she could remember was lying down on the bunk in the little room where she was being held.

Wait, yes, she could remember now. She had been given an injection of some sort. She had done some dope in her day, but she had never done anything like this. She couldn't remember a thing from the time she got the shot until this very moment.

She had been moved. Where was she now? And what was going on? Bunny tried to will the fogginess from her brain.

"Lights," someone said, and Bunny was blinded by a sudden, brilliant array of very bright lights.

"What is this?" she asked. "Who is here?"

Two beings materialized in the glare. She gasped when she saw them, for they were devils, with horns coming from the tops of their heads. Their skin was red, and they had long tails and cloven feet. Both devils were naked and both had huge erections.

"Oh, my Lord! Am I in hell?" she asked.

The beings moved toward her in a half crouch, sticking their tongues out as they approached. The tongues were unusually long and forked, and they seemed to flick and curl, like the tongue of a snake.

With every ounce of energy and willpower, Bunny tried to summon a scream, but was unable to utter a sound.

The two devils began licking her body with their long, forked tongues, flicking across her tightly drawn nipples, leaving a slimy trail of saliva down her stomach, probing her navel, then moving lower still, effecting a vaginal penetration that made her clitoris vibrate.

Amazingly, Bunny began experiencing paroxysms of ecstasy, even in the midst of her paralyzing fear.

First one devil, then the other, mounted her, pulling away as they finished, spraying white droplets of their malevolent seed onto her brown legs. When they were finished, the two devils left, walking away in the same, half-crouch, ape-like gait with which they had approached. For a moment, Bunny felt a sense of relief that the strange and terrifying ordeal was over. Then, appearing out of the glare of lights, was another figure, this one even more sinister and frightening than the devils.

He was wearing black boots, black leather pants, and black leather gloves. His torso was bare. He was a large, muscular man, but what made him appear even more frightening was the black hood he wore. Because of her drugged state, it took Bunny a moment to realize that he was dressed exactly like the executioners of medieval times. He came closer to her, then reached out to touch her, putting his leather-covered finger on the tip of one of her nipples. From there, he traced a path up to her neck, then, slowly, ran his finger from one side of her neck to the other. He looked at her through yellow eyes that were glowing with evil. Never in her life had Bunny experienced a more terrible sense of foreboding.

The masked man walked away from her, disappearing behind the blinding curtain of light. For a moment there was a sense of relief that he was gone, but that was short-lived for, a second later, he reappeared. Now, something was flashing in his hand, and when she saw what it was, she felt a sinking sensation in the pit of her stomach and a weakness in her knees. If she had not been held upright by the shackles that secured her, she would have fallen, for he was holding a double-headed executioner's ax.

Without any further preliminaries, he raised the axe, and whirled it around. Again, she saw a flash of light on the blade; then she felt a blow to the side of her neck; a slight stinging, followed by the sensation of falling. As her head tumbled to the floor, her last, conscious vision was of her own, headless body, still standing, but slumped in the shackles, pumping blood from the stump of her severed neck.

NINE

The video Don bought was of Annette Quinncannon. Though the tape was obviously professionally produced, there were no credits. That was understandable since nobody would want to be associated with an illegal tape. As a result, though the tape opened a window onto the investigation, it seemed to slam the door. They had nowhere to go from there.

"Maybe Bo Peep can help," Jenny suggested.

"How could she help?" Don asked.

"She's in the business," Jenny said. "She told us she had seen a thousand videos. Maybe—"

"She'll recognize something that will give us a lead," John said, interrupting. He smiled at Jenny. "Great idea, Jenny."

"Wet Spot Productions," Bo Peep said, less than two minutes into the video.

"You're sure?"

"Yes, I remember this picture from when we were carrying it. It was pulled because the actress was too young."

"What do you know about Wet Spot Productions?"

"I know it's owned by Tony Sarducci. He has one of the best production companies going. I mean, he really takes pride in his work. I'm sure he was upset when he found out this girl was underage."

"Do you know where I can find him?"

"Sarducci? Sure, his studio is in Burbank, on Palm Avenue."

"Thanks," John said.

"You aren't going to arrest him, are you?" Bo Peep said. She pointed to the screen. "I mean, look at that girl. Maybe she is underage, but if she is, it's just a matter of when her birthday is. She is as mature as any grown woman you'll see anywhere, and I'd be willing to bet that she has more experience than ninety percent of the women who are twice her age."

"I won't argue with you there," John said. "But that doesn't matter. The law says she is underage."

"So you are going to arrest him?"

"No," John said. "We aren't policemen. We are private detectives, hired by this girl's family. They are just trying to find her, that's all. They want her to come home."

"Then I hope you do find her," Bo Peep said in a plaintive voice. "Find her and take her home. It would be nice to go home to a place where you are wanted."

Don downloaded some of the scenes from the video they had been watching onto a three-and-a-half-inch floppy disk.

"By downloading these pictures, we are now technically guilty of kiddie porn," Don said as he took the disk from the computer.

"Yeah, I guess we are," John said. "We've been

technically guilty of a lot of things in the past, from assault to breaking and entering to violation of civil rights." He sighed. "But you know what? Somehow, of all those things, this one makes me feel the most queasy."

"I know what you mean," Don said. "But I don't see any other way of going from here."

"Nor do I."

It was decided that only John would make the pilgrimage to the Wet Spot Productions studios, where he would pass himself off as a distributor. Don was to stay back and do some computer applications that would bolster John's claim.

"How long before you will be ready?" John asked. Don's fingers were already flying across the keys. "I'll be ready by the time you need me," he promised.

Wet Spot Productions occupied a large brick building on Palm Avenue. It had been built originally as an auto dealership, and a barely discernible sign toward the back of the building displayed the faded image of a long, sleek, proud sedan with the boat-shaped prow and octagon logo of the Packard. "Ask the man who owns one," the ghostly image of a man in a fedora had been saying for nearly sixty years.

Despite the dated exterior, the inside had been extensively renovated, and John was surprised at how nice the office was. He had expected an element of sleaze, somewhat like the lobby of a flophouse hotel. Instead, this office was very appropriately decorated, with a deep pile maroon carpet, paneled walls, recessed lighting, and tasteful paintings.

Even the receptionist seemed incongruous with the business of adult videos, for she was an attractive middle-aged, well-dressed lady who could have been a bank executive. Sitting at an oversized mahogany desk, she touched her frosted hair and looked up as John approached, flashing him a big smile.

"Yes, sir, how may I help you?" she asked.

"I would like to see Tony Sarducci."

"And your name is?" the secretary asked as she pulled up the appointments page on her computer screen.

"Sal Todaro," John said. "I don't have an appointment."

The woman looked up from the screen. "Oh, I'm very sorry, Mr. Todaro. Mr. Sarducci doesn't see anyone without an appointment. Would you like me to see if I can make one for you?"

John shook his head. "I won't have time. I'm not going to be in town very long." He gave her his most appealing smile. "Do you think you could work me in between appointments? I do about half a million dollars a month in adult video distribution and I was hoping to do some business with Mr. Sarducci."

"Let me see what I can do. I'm sure he would be interested in seeing you. I'll call him."

"Thanks."

The woman spoke into the phone. "Mr. Sarducci, there is a man here who wants to meet with you. He says he is a distributor." The woman covered the mouthpiece with her hand. "What is the name of your company?"

"Todaro Video."

The woman repeated it into the phone, then said, "Yes, sir, I'll tell him." Hanging up, she flashed another smile toward John. "You can wait over there. Mr. Sarducci will be right out."

"Thank you."

John took a nearby seat, then picked up a copy of *Variety*. About five minutes later, someone came through the door. John looked up to see a man who was about five feet six inches tall, with a barrel chest that pulled at his jacket, broad shoulders, and thick arms. A cannonball-like head perched on the shoulders, apparently without benefit of a neck. He had thick lips, a flat, boxer's nose, yellowish-brown eyes, bushy eyebrows on a heavy brow ridge, and no hair.

"You Todaro?" the man asked.

"Yes. Mr. Sarducci?" John replied, standing and extending his hand.

"No. I'm Rodl, chief of security for Wet Spot Productions. Could I see some identification, please."

"I beg your pardon?"

"You have something that says you are who you say you are?"

"I have business cards," John said.

Rodl shook his head. "I need something with a picture. Like a driver's license."

"Oh, of course," John said, producing the Texas driver's license that Don had made for him.

Rodl examined the license and the business card for a minute, then nodded. "Wait here," he said. "Mr. Sarducci will see you in a moment."

John returned to the *Variety*.

A moment later another man came out to greet John. His smile was more professional than friendly, and he displayed very white, perfectly capped teeth. He was wearing a dark blue, open-neck silk shirt, with gold chains that sparkled against a bronzed chest.

"Mr. Todaro, I'm Tony Sarducci. Wanda tells me you are a distributor?"

"Yes. Todaro Video."

"And you say you are interested in doing business with me?"

"I am."

"Where is your operation?"

"I work out of Dallas. My area is the Southwest mostly; Texas, New Mexico, Arizona, Oklahoma, and Louisiana."

Another man came out of the back room then. He was a small man, with very pale skin, sparse blond hair, and watery blue eyes. Cupping his hand around Sarducci's ear, he whispered something. Sarducci nodded, then turned his attention back to John.

"Our Mr. Natas has just run a check on you, Mr. Todaro."

"You would be Mr. Natas, I take it?" John asked. Natas looked at John with a fixed, unblinking, expressionless stare.

"Yes, well, the thing is, he can find no mention of Todaro Video," Sarducci said.

"I would certainly hope he could find no mention of my company," John said. "It's costing me at least a million dollars a year to maintain that security."

Sarducci looked incredulous for a moment, then held up his finger. "Now, there is an interesting concept. Most distributors spend money to make the public aware of their services. Are you asking me to believe that you are spending money to keep your services quiet?"

"Absolutely. You see, my services are . . ." John paused for a moment before saying, "Rather unique. In fact, I do spend money to make people aware of my services, but I have to target my advertising to a very specific clientele, if you know what I mean."

Sarducci shook his head. "No, Mr. Todaro, I don't know what you mean."

"Actually, I think you *do* know what I mean." John took a floppy disk from his jacket pocket. "May I use one of your computers for a moment?" he asked. "Perhaps this will explain."

Sarducci nodded toward the computer that was on Wanda's desk.

"No," John said. "I don't think you want to look at this out here."

Sarducci stroked his chin for a moment, then nodded at Mr. Natas. The little man used a magnetic card to swipe through the electronic lock-pad, opening the door to the back. "Come with us," Sarducci said.

Just beyond the door was a long hallway with several offices off either side of the hall. At the far end of the hall a big picture window opened onto a large room. Though his view of the room was somewhat limited, John could see light racks and camera stands on the other side, so he knew he was looking into a studio.

"In here," Sarducci said, opening the door to one of the rooms. "You may use that computer."

John sat down behind the computer, turned it on, then slid his floppy into the disk drive. He opened the first picture, that of two girls engaged in a sexual act. The girls looked like high school girls.

"Do you recognize this scene?" John asked.

"Why should I recognize it?" Sarducci asked.

"Because you produced it."

"I would never produce such a picture," Sarducci insisted. "Those girls are obviously under-age." He looked at Mr. Natas. "Wouldn't you say those two girls are underage, Mr. Natas?"

"Yes," Mr. Natas said. That was the first time John heard him speak, and his "yes" emerged as a sibilant hiss.

"Oh, I agree, they are underage," John said. He brought up another image. "I particularly like this one, don't you?"

"What are trying to do, Mr. Todaro?" Sarducci asked.

"I thought it was rather obvious," John said as still a third image appeared on the screen. "I'm trying to do business with you."

"And you think I do this kind of business?"

"Well, let me put it this way. I think I could make it exceptionally lucrative for you if you did do this kind of business," John said. "But if you don't, then I am obviously wasting my time and yours." He closed the file, then started to get up.

"You know what I think?" Natas said. "I don't think you are who you say you are. I think you are trying to run some sort of sting operation."

"I'll show you our Web site," John said. He clicked on an Internet icon, then looked up. "What's your password to get onto the Net?"

"It's—" Sarducci said, then stopped and chuckled. "Nice try. If you really want to get on, I'll get you on."

John made a point of raising his hands from the keyboard. "It's all yours."

"Get up and turn your back."

With Mr. Natas making certain he didn't try to steal the password by watching Sarducci's fingers, John turned his back to the computer. He heard the keystrokes behind him, then the dialing, and finally the clicks, buzz, and rush of connection.

"You're on-line," Sarducci said.

John returned to the keyboard, hoping he had given Don time to complete everything. In the address bar he typed Todaro Video. A few seconds later a very sophisticated-looking Web page came up.

"Here it is," John said. "This is my company."

Sarducci looked at the page.

"Todaro Video, featuring classic movies from the thirties, forties, and fifties," the home page said.

"What is this, some kind of joke?" Sarducci asked.

"Click onto the harlequin," John said.

"What are you talking about? That's not a link. You can tell a link by looking at it."

"Try it."

Sarducci did as instructed and the screen went black.

"What the hell? The screen went black."

"It will stay that way until you type in the password."

"How do you do that? There's not even a cursor." He struck a few keys, but nothing happened. "See what I mean?"

"Hit escape, delete, escape."

Sarducci did as instructed, and a cursor appeared.

"Now, type the word 'buGGer,' with a small b and two capital g's."

Sarducci typed the password and the black disappeared.

"You have entered a secret chamber known but to the most discriminating pleasure seekers in the world of erotica. Our titillating offerings, while never mundane, are not for

the squeamish. They are especially created for those with the most refined and eclectic sexual tastes. Tell us what you want, and your order will be filled within seven days."

Sarducci looked up at John in surprise. "I've never heard of this," he said.

"You weren't meant to," John replied. "As I'm sure you can understand, we must be very, very careful about who we let into our circle. Once in, however, the reward for membership is very, very great."

"Mr. Todaro, I don't know what you are intimating," Sarducci said. "I produce adult videos. Now, while they may not be something you would rent for your Aunt Tillie, they are absolutely legal. So, what is it you want?"

"I'm sure you have figured that out by now," John said.

"Perhaps he is talking about our special films division," Natas suggested.

Sarducci put his hands up and shook his head. "I don't have anything to do with that operation."

"Let me get this straight," John said. "You aren't denying that your company produces such films, only that you have anything to do with it. Is that right?"

Sarducci looked at Natas. "You handle this, Mr. Natas. I have some business to take care of." Sarducci left the office. John heard the door to the studio open and close.

"Is he serious?" John asked.

"That isn't the question, Mr. Todaro. The question is, are you serious?" Natas replied.

"Yes."

"And what, exactly, are you asking for?"

"What, exactly, is your special films division prepared to do?"

"Until I can check you out, Mr. Todaro, this conversation has gone as far as it can go," Natas said.

John punched out the floppy disk he had brought, and put it in his shirt pocket. "I'm sorry to hear that," he said. "I'm sure our business venture would have been mutually profitable. I'm sorry if I took up too much of your time." John started toward the door.

"What? Wait!" Natas called to him. "It's just a matter of good business sense, that's all. I'm sure you understand."

"Oh, yes, I understand," John said. He wagged his finger. "But my understanding isn't critical here. Yours is."

"What do you mean by that?" Natas asked.

"No matter who you ask, even if it is someone I do a great deal of business with, they are going to tell you that they have never heard of me," John said. "They are going to say that because they well understand the penalty for saying otherwise. If anyone ever mentions my name, or the name of my company to anyone else, they will be forever barred from doing business with me again. Call anyone you want, verify me in any way you can, but it will be too late. The deal is on the table now, and now only. Take it or leave it."

"How much money are we talking?" Natas asked.

"Good day, Mr. Natas," John said, turning away one more time.

"Wait! All right," Natas said. "If you are that careful about your operation, perhaps I don't need to check you out. While you are protecting yourself, you would be protecting me as well. If the money is right, I think we can do business."

"Good," John said without smiling. "I'll be in touch very soon. Have a good day, Mr. Natas."

* * *

When John returned to the office that he, Jenny, and Don were occupying, he smiled at their questioning faces.

"Here it is," he said, taking the disk from his pocket and handing it to Don.

"Here is what?" Jenny asked. "I don't understand."

"I embedded a pirate program on the screen," Don explained. "When they went onto the Internet they typed in the password that granted them access. If my program performed properly, we just stole that password."

Don slid the disk into the computer, then tapped a few keys. Six asterisks appeared on the screen.

"It didn't work, did it?" Jenny asked. "I mean, all it got was the asterisks."

"Wait," Don said. He typed a few more keys, then took his hands away from the keyboard. Under the first asterisk, a series of letters began to appear as, automatically, the computer started running through the alphabet. Finally the rapidly rolling letters under the first asterisk stopped changing. The letter "S" remained. The same sequence was repeated under the second asterisk until the letter "u" appeared.

"Jeez," Jenny said as she watched the process. "You didn't need this sophisticated program. These assholes have so little imagination that I've already broken it."

"What is it?" John asked.

"Sucker," Jenny said.

No sooner had Jenny spoken the word than the third letter, a "c," popped up.

"She's right," John said. "We don't need you, Don," he teased.

The program finished its run and, as Jenny had predicted, the password was "Sucker."

"Now, let's see what we can find out," Don said, clicking on the Internet icon. When prompted, he typed in the password and was on-line.

"You're there," Jenny said.

Another click took them to the mailbox.

"Hello, look at this," Don said. He pointed to a "mail sent" letter, with the subject listed as "New Market."

"Let's read it," John said.

Don opened the letter, then chuckled.

"What is it?"

"They are smarter than I thought they were. The mail is encrypted."

"Can you break it?"

"I think I can," Don said confidently. "Just let me work on it for a while."

Open field,
East Hollywood

At the corner of Bixel and Second Street, an empty lot occupied the space where there had once stood a large building. The building had burned down three years earlier, and some dispute on the insurance had delayed its rebuilding. As a result, what had been a thriving grocery store and parking lot was now an ugly scar, an unkempt field that was overgrown with weeds and sprinkled with broken bottles, old cans, cardboard boxes, and paper.

Benny Mason and Ray Kelly, both twelve years old, often used the field as a shortcut. Their parents had cautioned them against using the field because there were so many broken bottles lying in the weeds that there was a danger they could cut themselves badly. But, as children are wont to do, the boys ignored the warning.

It was just before four o'clock and the two boys were on the way home. Benny was carrying a football and as they started across the field, he brought the ball back to throw a pass.

"Go long!" he shouted.

Ray started running across the field while Benny provided the play-by-play description.

"Kelly is streaking down the sidelines, Mason is in the pocket, he looks off the first receiver, looks off the second, he sees Kelly and throws the bomb!"

Benny threw the ball, leading Ray perfectly. Ray made the grab, then, holding his hand out as if stiff-arming, picked his way through the imaginary USC defenders as he headed toward the goal.

"He's at the thirty, he's at the twenty, he's at the ten," Benny shouted.

Suddenly Ray went down.

"He's down! How could you go down when there is nobody there to tackle you?" Benny asked, laughing, and starting toward Ray.

"Ahhhhhh!" Ray suddenly screamed. He jumped up and ran toward Benny. "Benny, it's—it's—" Ray stammered.

"Ray, what is it?" Benny asked. Ray's scream, and the expression on his face, had frightened Benny.

"It's a woman," Ray said, pointing to the place where he fell. "I tripped over her."

"You tripped over a woman?"

"She's dead," Ray said. "She—she ain't got no head!"

* * *

Within half an hour there were several people gathered in the field: two police photographers, one for still photos and one with a video camera; two people from the medical examiner's office; a newspaper reporter; some people from Homicide; and a couple of uniformed policemen. Yellow tape marked the perimeter of the crime scene, and at least three dozen curious onlookers were on the other side of the tape. Three cars and a hearse had driven across the field, picking their way through the refuse as best they could. Now these same cars and the hearse sat nearby. The cars were all painted black and white and emblazoned with LAPD logos. In addition, they were decorated with red and blue lights. In one of the cars the police radio was turned up loud enough that the carrier wave could be heard. The rushing sound was frequently interrupted when the squelch was broken and the disembodied voice of a female dispatcher began providing instructions in a dry, monotone voice.

One of the policemen who had been called to the scene was Lieutenant Homer Jackson from the Hollywood Station. He parked his car on the edge of the field and began picking his way through the tall weeds. Before he got to the scene, he was met by one of the uniformed police officers who were watching over the scene.

"You're Lieutenant Jackson?"

"Yes."

"I heard you were coming down to take a look around. I'm Patrolman Riggs."

"What can you tell me, Riggs?" Jackson asked.

"Not much yet. The body is that of an African American female, probably between twenty-five and thirty-five."

"How do you know she was African American?" Jackson asked.

"Beg your pardon?" the patrolman replied, surprised by the question.

"You said she was African American. How do know that?"

Patrolman Riggs was obviously confused by the inquiry, coming as it did from a police officer who was himself an African American. "Well, uh, I mean, you can see that she is African American," Riggs stammered.

Lieutenant Jackson shook his head. "No, you can't see that," he explained. "All you can see is that she is black. For all you know, she could have been Cuban, Haitian, Mexican, or Jamaican, none of which would qualify her as African American."

"I guess I hadn't thought of that," Riggs said. He smiled. "I just didn't want to offend you."

"Don't be such a slave to political correctness that you call everyone you see with black skin an African American. It is more important to be accurate than to be politically correct."

Riggs laughed nervously. "Yes, sir, I see what you mean," he said.

"Who called in the report?"

"She was found by a couple of young boys," Riggs replied. "They were cutting through this field."

"Hell of a thing for kids to have to find," Jackson said. "Are they all right?"

"I think they are going to be okay. They are with a counselor now," Riggs explained. "You want to talk to them?"

Jackson shook his head. "No need," he said. "They've been traumatized enough. I'll just read their statements. What else do you have?" Jackson asked.

"Not much, I'm afraid. We figure she's a hooker; otherwise we would've gotten a missing person's report. This poor creature just turned up."

By now, Jackson had reached the body and he stood there, looking down at the light brown skin of the headless torso of a young, black woman. "Jesus," he said.

"As you can see," Riggs continued, "they cut off her hands so we wouldn't be able to identify her by her fingerprints."

"I think I know who it is," Lieutenant Jackson said.

"Really?" the uniformed patrolman asked in surprise.

Jackson squatted down beside the body, then pointed to her feet. "See if she has a rabbit tattooed on her right ankle."

Riggs lifted her right leg. There, on the inside of her ankle, was a small, blue rabbit. "Hey, you're right," Riggs said in admiration.

"I wish I had been wrong," Jackson said solemnly.

"Well, well, look at our little Bunny now," Wallace said. "So much for having a good head on her shoulders." He laughed.

"Wallace, you have a sick-assed sense of humor," Jackson said.

"Yeah, I guess I do," Wallace agreed. "But I can't help it, I've always liked black humor." He laughed again. "Black humor, damn, I'm on a roll today, aren't I?"

"What are you doing down here anyway? You're Vice, this is Homicide."

"I know," Wallace said. He pointed to Bunny's body. "But I feel sort of a proprietary interest in her. She's one of my own, an alumna, so to speak. And when some sicko bastard takes out one of my people, I take a personal interest. Have you got anything?"

"Nothing so far," Jackson replied.

"Tell you what, I'll keep my eyes and ears open with my people," Wallace said. "If I hear anything helpful, I'll let you know."

"I appreciate it."

TEN

Wearing visitors' badges, John and Jenny worked their way through the crowded Hollywood Community Police Station. They were there in answer to an invitation from Lieutenant Jackson. Although it was issued as an invitation, it was worded in a fashion that let John know it could quite easily be followed by a court summons. To avoid any confrontation with the local police, John had decided to respond to the invitation, at least to a point. The invitation had asked for all three to come to the station, but John left Don Yee back at the motel, working with the computer, trying to crack the encryption code that was being used by Wet Spot Productions.

The name tags John and Jenny were issued allowed them access through the warrenlike halls and passageways of the police station. Finally, following a second, and only slightly less garbled, set of directions, they pushed through a double door and found who they were looking for.

Lieutenant Jackson was sitting at his desk. His jacket was off and draped across the back of his chair, leaving his .38 police special and his gold-and-blue badge clearly visible. At first, Jackson didn't notice his visitors, his attention being riv-

eted on the little cardboard box of Chinese take-
out he held in his left hand. In his right hand,
a pair of deftly wielded chopsticks snapped open
and shut over the top of the box. Seeing the two
coming toward him, Jackson put the box and
chopsticks down. He poked a dangling bean
sprout into his mouth, then sucked on the ends
of his fingers.

"I thought there were three of you."

"That's right," John replied.

"Where's the other one? I asked for all three of
you to come."

"He couldn't make it," John replied, as if that
were all the answer he needed.

Lieutenant Jackson sighed, realizing that was all
the answer he was going to get. "All right, before
we get started here, I want to know just who in
the hell you people are?" he finally asked.

"You know who we are. You sent for us," John
replied.

"I did," Lieutenant Jackson said. Opening
the middle drawer of his desk, he removed a
manilla envelope and dropped a rather sub-
stantial file onto the desk in front of him. He
had obviously been doing his homework. "This
is your file."

"That's a pretty big file," John insisted. "You
should know us pretty well by now."

"It's a big file, all right, but it doesn't tell me
much. I know who all of you were, but I don't
know who you *are*. I know you are not private
security people. At least, not like any private security people I've ever had anything to do with."

"Why is it important that you know who we
are?" Jenny asked.

"Let's just say that I suffer from the same disease

that killed the cat. I'm curious, and I'm figuring you are with some government agency, though what agency it might be, I have no idea."

Jackson paused, waiting for some reply, but none was forthcoming.

He sighed in frustration. "All right, I can see the direct approach isn't going to get me any farther than my background checks did," he said. "So we may as well get on with it. I do appreciate your coming."

"You said you had some information on the case we are working," John said.

Lieutenant Jackson ran his hand over the top of his head. "I do have something that might be related," he said.

"What is it?"

"First, let me ask you this. When is the last time either of you saw Bunny Miller?"

"A few days ago," Jenny answered. "Though we have talked to her on the phone since then."

Jackson looked interested. "You talked to her on the phone? When was that?"

"Night before last."

"About what time?"

"What is this all about, Lieutenant Jackson?" John asked. "Has Bunny turned up missing?"

"You might say that," Jackson replied. "At least part of her is missing."

"*Part* of her?" Jenny asked, confused by Lieutenant Jackson's strange remark.

"Yes. We have her body, but her head is missing." He stood up. "Come to the morgue with me. I don't have any idea what you are involved with, but I think you should see this."

* * *

"Jesus, what sort of sicko son of a bitch would do something like this?" Jenny asked as she, John, and Lieutenant Jackson stood in the morgue, looking down at the slab on which lay the headless, handless body of a young, light-skinned black woman.

"Are you positive this is Bunny?" John asked.

"Yes," Jackson said.

"I must say, it looks like her to me," Jenny replied. "I spent enough time with her to recognize her, even like this."

Lieutenant Jackson pointed to the tattoo. "That's how we identified her. That rabbit was her trademark."

"Have you had many mutilation murders like this before?" John asked.

Lieutenant Jackson shook his head. "This is the only one I'm aware of. Listen, I don't know what you folks are up to, who you are working for, or even if what you are doing is legitimate. But I have a feeling that whatever it is you are involved in has something to do with Bunny's death."

"Whoa, wait a minute! You don't think *we're* the bad guys, do you?" Jenny asked, surprised by the thought.

Jackson shook his head. "No, I don't think you are the bad guys. But I don't think you are doing everything by the book either."

John chuckled. "You've got that right, Lieutenant Jackson. You don't even want to *see* the book we use."

"That's what I thought," Jackson said. He looked around the morgue to see if there was anyone close enough to overhear him. "That's why I want to help."

"You want to help?"

"Yes. Whether you are working inside the law or out, if your mission turns up the scum who did this, then you can count on my support. Call on me anytime you need my help."

"Thanks," John said.

When they returned to their car, Jenny saw a white envelope pinned by the wiper to the windshield. She lifted up the wiper, retrieved the envelope, and extracted the letter, then read it, curious as to what it might be.

"What is it?"

"It just says *Oval Orifice,*" Jenny said.

"Oval Office?"

"Orifice," Jenny corrected. "Those are the only two words written here."

"*Oval Orifice.* Do you have any idea what that means?" John asked.

Jenny shook her head.

When they returned to the motel, they found Don hard at work behind the computer.

"How are you making out?" John asked.

"I am making progress, slowly but surely," Don replied. He pointed to the computer screen. "I sent an e-mail letter to Wet Spot Productions. They have an encryption macro so it promptly encoded my letter. And, since I know what my letter said, I have been able to break most of the code by reversing the procedure."

"Just most of it?" John asked.

"Well, it would appear they have a sliding matrix so that the letter combinations won't always line up. However, I have been able to decipher at least eighty percent of it, and that's enough to get a feel of what is going on."

"So what is going on?"

"The special films division is called Satan, and it appears to be the gateway to every sexual perversion you can possibly imagine," Don said. "Real sleazy, scumbag shit, from kiddie porn to bestiality to bondage to golden shower to S&M. Oh, and I do have some addresses for you, if you are interested."

"Yes, I am interested," John said. "Oh, and while you are at it, you might check this out as well." He handed the paper with the words *Oval Orifice* to Don.

"Ha. Funny title," Don said, looking at the paper.

John and Jenny looked at each other. Obviously, *Oval Orifice was* a title, though until this moment, that fact had escaped them. It took Don to figure it out.

Even though John hadn't touched anything, he knew he was going to have to take a very hot shower when he got back to the motel room. He had been in every cesspool and garbage pit in half the cities of the world, but right here, in Los Angeles, less than a mile from some of the most glamorous and expensive real estate in the world, was one of the sleaziest areas he had ever seen.

The men and women who plied the streets were the scum of the earth. They had multicolored, spiked hair, tattoos over half their bodies, pierced body parts, and lots of leather and chains. John was propositioned at least four times, and for at least two of the propositions, he hadn't known if they were male or female.

Often, as he passed alleys and door openings, he would get a whiff of marijuana. A couple of times he saw people doing a line of coke, and once he even saw someone shooting up.

John turned up one of the alleys, then stopped at a door that was almost blocked from view by a large trash Dumpster. There were no pictures or signs to indicate that a business might be beyond the door, but there was a hand-painted number, and the number matched one of the numbers Don had given him.

John pushed the door open and found himself standing inside a long, narrow hallway. One yellowed lightbulb hung from a cord at the far end. The other end of the hallway was shut off, not by a door, but by a hanging curtain. When John started toward the curtain, a man stepped through it. He was wearing a sleeveless shirt, dirty jeans, and a wide leather belt with a huge buckle. A large swastika was tattooed on one forearm; a dagger, dripping blood, was on the other. A P-38 pistol nestled in the shoulder holster he was wearing.

"What do you want?" the man asked.

"I'm looking for a video," John replied.

"What kind of video?"

"I like the things Satan has done," John said.

"Are you a policeman?"

"No."

"Come on."

The man stepped back through the curtain, then held it open for John. John nodded at him, then went inside.

The room was long and narrow, not much wider than the hallway had been. The walls were bare brick and the windows were high and small. In contrast to the well-lit and artfully presented racks tended by Bo Peep and Bambi in Eros Entertainment, there was nothing in here but long tables piled with videos. Half-a-dozen bare lightbulbs, similar to the one hanging in the hall, provided the light.

John started to pick up one of the videos.

"Don't touch," a man with a terribly pocked face said. "If you want to see something, tell me and I'll show it to you." Like the big man who had shown him into the room, this man was armed.

"How do I know what I want if I can't see what the tapes are?" John replied.

"You tell me what you want, I'll find it. We have young stuff, extreme S&M, beastiality."

"What do you have by Satan?"

The pock-faced man pointed to three tapes. "These three."

"Can I look at the titles?"

"I'll read the titles to you," the pock-faced man said. Picking up the tapes one at a time, he began to read: *"Junior High Pussy, Tits in a Bind, Ride the Pony."* He put them back down.

"I'll take all three," John said. He started to reach for the tapes, but the pock-faced man pulled his pistol. "Pigmeat!" he shouted. "Over here!"

At the pock-faced man's shout, the others who were standing by the table moved quickly away. The muscular man in the sleeveless shirt ambled over.

"What is it?" Pigmeat asked.

"I think we have us a ringer here. He wants kiddie, S&M, and animals."

"What are you doin' here, mister?" Pigmeat asked.

"Nothing," John said. "I'm just looking for a little entertainment, that's all."

"Uh-uh," Pigmeat said, shaking his head. "You might like blondes, redheads, brunettes, white, black, or Asian. But someone who is into the specialty arts don't generally cross over. When you say you want all three, that rings a bell somewhere, you know what I mean?"

"All right, I'll just take one of them," John said. Pigmeat shook his head, then cocked his weapon. "Mister, you ain't getting any of them. I think you'd better get out now, while you still can."

John took to heart Pigmeat's lesson. He visited four other underground video outlets that night, buying samples of all, but being very careful to select only one kind at each store.

John, Don, and Jenny spent the rest of the night watching the videos. Some of the kiddie porn featured children who weren't even through puberty. The extreme S&M was brutal, complete with floggings with cat-o'-nine tails and piercing of nipples, labia, foreskin, and testicles. In one picture it looked exactly like a young woman's nipples had been chopped off, leaving gaping holes oozing blood. But the same girl was seen in three other videos, so they knew it was special effects.

The bestiality pictures featured jackasses, ponies, and dogs. They were obviously looped to make it appear as if the animals were engaged in lengthy sex when it was obvious they had no real interest in the prospect.

"Damn," Jenny said when the last tape had been viewed. "Next time you fellas take a girl out to a movie, see if you can't select a nice musical."

"Yeah, I know what you mean," John said. He pointed to the pile of porn tapes. "It's hard to believe that anyone, anywhere, could actually get off on that shit."

* * *

The video cost Uncle Billy five hundred dollars. He had always paid a premium for his videos, simply because his particular taste was difficult to satisfy, but he had never paid this much for one.

"It will be worth it, believe me," Uncle Billy's special video dealer told him.

Taking the video home, Uncle Billy locked the door to his house, then went over to the window and looked outside. His next-door neighbor, Mrs. Etta Claire Clark, was in the backyard, working in her flower garden.

Uncle Billy didn't care much for Mrs. Clark. The old busybody was a nosy troublemaker. There had been an unpleasant incident three months ago, when Mrs. Clark accused him of molesting her ten-year-old granddaughter.

It was a false accusation, because he hadn't done anything to the little girl. All he had done was come over to speak to her while she was swimming in her grandmother's pool. He was just trying to be nice to her, to be a friendly neighbor.

The problem occurred when he touched her. He had not meant it to be a touch with any sexual intent. It was all quite accidental. He had merely steadied her as she was climbing out of the pool. He had put his hands on her chest. It was mostly little-girl flat, though with nipples that were slightly protruding little bulbs, pregnant with the promise of future breasts.

That inconsequential touch had given him an instant erection, the palms of his hands had grown sweaty, and his breathing had become irregular. Of course he didn't follow up on it, wouldn't have, couldn't have, under the circumstances.

But somehow that evil bitch, Mrs. Clark, had seen through all that. Almost witchlike, she'd seemed to know what he wanted, what he was thinking, and she'd reported him to the police.

Uncle Billy had a record as a child sex offender, so the police were quick to respond to Mrs. Clark's complaint. But because nothing had actually happened, and because the little girl wasn't as astute at reading Uncle Billy's mind as was Mrs. Clark, there was no offense they could book him on.

"If I ever find something I can make stick on you, I'll do it," one of the policemen told him. "I have a ten-year-old daughter and I'm just looking to break the head of some perverted bastard like you."

Ever since that time Uncle Billy was extremely careful about watching any of his videos. If Mrs. Clark ever happened to look into his apartment, and he was sure she was just the kind of person who would do something like that, she could cause him a lot of trouble if she reported what he was watching. It seemed safe enough now, though. She was on the far side of her backyard, on her hands and knees, weeding her flowers.

Uncle Billy smiled, then returned to his lounge chair, picked up the remote, turned on the TV, then clicked on the VCR.

The picture opened with a black screen. Then, in Old English lettering, the titles began to roll in bright red, appearing only long enough to be read, then dissolving and sliding down the screen as drops of blood.

A Satan Production
Rabbit Chop

The first scene in the video showed two hooded men leading a young black woman across the room. Turning her around, they lifted her arms over her head, then fastened her to shackles on the wall. She seemed to be dazed and she hung there for a moment, her head slumped forward, almost as if she were unconscious.

"What is this?" Uncle Billy asked aloud.

This woman was clearly of legal age. She looked to be at least twenty-two or twenty-three. This was very disappointing. This wasn't at all what he'd thought he was getting. And he had paid five hundred dollars for the video.

The first two men left; then two more men appeared. They were made up to resemble devils, complete with red skin, horns, long tails, and cloven feet. Moving in a crouch, chimpanzee-like, they began jumping around, looking at her with beastly grins. Then they began licking all over her body with long, narrow, forked tongues. Uncle Billy had to admit that whoever the makeup artist was, he was very good. The two cavorting creatures were very realistic-looking.

Both creatures had sex with the captive woman, pulling out just in time to spray their semen on her. Some might get off on this, Uncle Billy thought, but this was not the kind of thing he could enjoy. On the contrary, there was something very disconcerting about this picture, and he felt extremely uneasy as he watched it. He wanted to turn it off, and more than once he picked up the remote to do so, but for some strange reason, he could not.

Uncle Billy was mesmerized by the scenes unfolding before him. He was mesmerized, but he was not sexually aroused. In fact, the erection he'd had at the beginning of the film had long since gone away. He felt no sexual stimulation at all, but he still could not turn away from this very disturbing video.

On screen the two devils left, to be replaced by another man. This man was wearing a black hood and black pants. He was bare from the waist up and Uncle Billy could see that, though he wasn't terribly tall, he was powerfully built, with a deep chest and wide shoulders. His arms were so heavily muscled that he had to hold them out from his sides.

The man walked up to the young black captive woman and ran his gloved hand across her breasts, then up to her neck. After that, he stepped out of the picture. For a moment, there was a very close picture of the young woman's face, showing the fear and confusion in her eyes.

Uncle Billy gasped. He knew this girl! She was a prostitute who worked the area he sometimes visited. He had never been with her, she was too old for him, but he definitely recognized her.

The hooded man reappeared, this time carrying a new prop. It looked very much like a headsman's ax, no doubt similar to the ax that had been used to behead King Henry's Queen Anne.

On screen, the hooded man swung the ax around one time, then quickly and cleanly, chopped off the girl's head. It tumbled forward as her body sagged in the shackles and blood gushed from the wound in her neck.

"Oh, my God!" Uncle Billy shouted, just before the unchecked vomit spewed from his mouth like a volcano in eruption.

Badly shaken, Uncle Billy washed his face and hands, ran water over his head, then put on a clean shirt and returned to his den. The video had automatically rewound and ejected, and was now projecting halfway from the player. Uncle Billy looked at it for a long moment, trying to decide what to do with it.

He was sure it wasn't real, but it was so realistic-looking that there was no way he would ever watch it again. How could anyone derive any sexual satisfaction from that kind of picture? *There are some sick people in the world,* he thought.

Finally, after he got over the disgust and uneasiness of the picture, he began to get angry. He had paid five hundred dollars for that thing. It was, by far, the most expensive video he had ever purchased, and the most disturbing. He had not bought the video to be disturbed; he had bought it to be sexually aroused. It certainly had not done that. In fact, the more he thought about it, the angrier he got. He called his contact.

"Yeah?" the voice grunted from the other end.

"This is Uncle Billy."

"What can I do for you?"

"The video you sold me today wasn't what I wanted. Who wants to see a video of a black girl getting her head chopped off?"

There was a pause from the other end. "What are you talking about this shit on the phone for? You crazy or something? I don't know what you are talking about."

"I'm talking about the video I got from you today," Uncle Billy started to say, but before he could finish his sentence, the phone went dead.

That angered Uncle Billy even more. All right, if they wouldn't talk to him on the phone, they would talk to him in person. Uncle Billy decided then and there that he would return this video, and get his money back. He might also make them give him a free video to compensate for the trouble they had caused him.

Marina Del Rey

Uncle Billy wished now that he hadn't come. It was after dark, a heavy fog had moved in off the ocean, and now the warehouse and docks were covered in a shroud that was so thick that he could barely see the hood ornament of his car. He was reduced to driving at a speed no faster than he could walk.

In addition to the blackness of the night and the density of the fog, his windshield became completely opaque when his wipers failed. With a curse of frustration, Uncle Billy lowered his door window, then stuck his head out in order to be able to see ahead. He could hear the muffled clanging of a buoy-bell and the mournful sound of a foghorn.

He was lost.

He knew he had bought the video down here, somewhere, but in the dark and the fog he was unable to see the landmarks. He gave up any idea of returning the video. Now all he wanted to do was go back home, so he turned onto a road that he thought was the right one to take him out of there.

His initial anger had turned to frustration over not being able to find the place right away. That frustration turned to apprehension, then into a full-blown anxiety attack. He shouldn't have come.

"Oh!" he shouted aloud when suddenly, in front of him, he saw the black-and-yellow stripes of a road barricade. Not only was this the wrong road, had he continued on it, he would have driven off into the water. Fortunately he was not going very fast, and he was able to stop the car in time.

A car pulled up behind him and stopped.

"Now what," Uncle Billy said.

The car just sat there.

Uncle Billy stuck his head out the window. "This is a dead end!" he shouted.

The car behind him didn't move.

"You are going to have to back up!" Uncle Billy shouted again. "We can't go any farther this way."

When the car still didn't move, Uncle Billy shifted into reverse, hoping that when the driver behind him saw the backup lights come on, he would move and give Uncle Billy room to get out.

The car behind him began backing, and Uncle Billy breathed a sigh of relief. It was working.

Uncle Billy and the car behind him were both backing up, and had just about made it out when the car behind him stopped again.

Uncle Billy leaned out the window again, and had started to shout to the car behind him when to his surprise, then fear, the car moved forward and began pushing him.

"Hey, wait! What are you doing?" Uncle Billy shouted. Reflexively, he put on the brakes, but the pavement was slickened by the fog and the brakes didn't stop his car from moving. He pushed harder on the brakes, but it didn't help. The car slipped down a steep, concrete embankment into a deep culvert.

The rear end of the car crunched into the bottom of the culvert; then the front end slammed around as well. Panic-stricken, Uncle Billy got out of the car and tried to climb up the side of the embankment, but it was too steep. He tried several more times, but each time he slipped back down.

Then he remembered the cell phone. He went back to the car and reached inside.

"You looking for this?" a man asked, holding up the phone.

"What?" Uncle Billy asked. "How did you get down here?"

"I climbed down when I saw your car go over the edge."

"You saw what happened up there? That fool pushed me—" Uncle Billy said, then stopped. "Wait a minute, I know you. What are you harassing me for? I haven't done anything."

"Where is the video?"

"What?"

"Come, come, Uncle Billy. You and I both know you have a video you shouldn't have."

"It's not what you think," Uncle Billy said. "Really, it's not kiddie porn. Well, you can see for yourself. I mean, take it with you and look at it, you'll see that it isn't kiddie porn."

"Where is the video?" the man asked again.

"It's there, on top of the dashboard. Take it. I want you to take it. You'll see what I'm talking about."

When the man raised his other hand, Uncle Billy saw that he was holding a pistol.

"What?" Uncle Billy asked in total shock. "What are you doing? I told you, I haven't done anything!"

The silencer and the fog muffled the shots so effectively that even had someone been walking by at the top of the culvert at that time, they would have thought only that they heard a twig snap somewhere. Three times.

Sunset Motel

"That was some fog we had last night," Jenny said as she poured herself a cup of coffee.

"Yeah," John said. "Like the poet said, it was the kind of fog that crept in on little cat's feet."

Jenny looked at the box of doughnuts, only three of which remained. "I thought you were going to get two dozen doughnuts this morning."

"I did," John said. He nodded toward Don, who was sitting at the computer, working the mouse with one hand and holding a doughnut in the other. "The problem is, the human disposal unit over there got into them before we did."

"Research like this uses up a lot of mental energy," Don said, his words muffled by the fact that he had his mouth full of doughnut. "If you want results, you have to keep me fed."

"It would take a fully staffed mess hall to keep you fed," Jenny joked. She picked up one of the three remaining doughnuts and sat in a chair near the window. "John, do you think Annette is alive?"

"I don't know," John replied. "I'm beginning to fear the worst. If she were alive, I'm almost sure we would have run into her by now. I'm bothered by the fact that it has been a while since those who did know her last saw her."

"Prostitution is a high-risk business," Jenny said. "It always has been. She could have been murdered by one of her johns, killed by a pimp, or even OD'd."

The phone rang.

"Yeah," John said into the phone, purposely making his answer vague.

"Mr. Barrone, this is Lieutenant Jackson. I told

you that from time to time I might have some in-formation for you? Well, this is one of those times."

"What do you have?"

"I believe in your investigation out here you have dealt with a man named Marvin Fry?"

John had to stop and think for a moment.

"Perhaps you know him as Uncle Billy."

"Yes," John said. "Uncle Billy, I know who you are talking about."

"He was found dead down in the waterfront dis-trict last night."

"What was the cause of death?" When both Jenny and Don looked at him questioningly, John realized they might think he was talking about Annette. He mouthed the words "Uncle Billy." They nodded in understanding.

"He was shot."

"Shot?"

"Yes. And there is more."

"What more?"

"We found something in the car," Lieutenant Jackson said. "Something that I think you are go-ing to want to see."

"What?"

"I don't think I want to talk about it over the phone. Maybe you'd better come down to the sta-tion."

"We'll be right there."

When John, Jenny, and Don asked for visitors' passes at the police station, they were treated with professional courtesy and shown directly to a desk marked VISITING OFFICERS.

"We have CIA, FBI, NSA, and Federal Marshal

passes," the desk lieutenant said, opening his desk drawer. "Which will it be?"

"We're sort of at-large," John said.

The desk lieutenant chuckled. "You feds and your secrecy," he said. He took three clip-on passes from the drawer. "All right," he said. "Here are three different badges, one for each of you. Take your pick."

John picked up the badge marked CIA.

"Ha! I knew you were CIA," the desk sergeant said.

"Or, I might be FBI but wanted to throw you off," John suggested.

The desk lieutenant stroked his jaw. "Yeah," he said. "Yeah, you might be at that. I didn't think of that."

When all three were properly checked in, they found their way back to Lieutenant Jackson's desk. He greeted them, then handed them a heavy brown envelope.

"You didn't get this from me," he said.

"What is it?"

"It's the copy of a video that was found in Uncle Billy's car."

"Kiddie porn?" Jenny asked.

Lieutenant Jackson shook his head. "I wish," he said. "This is worse. Far worse."

"Wait a minute," John said. "What could possibly be worse than a kiddie-porn video?"

"A snuff film," Lieutenant Jackson replied.

"You mean there really is such a thing? I thought snuff films were a myth."

"It may have started that way, but this is very real," Jackson said.

"How do you know it is a snuff film?"

"Because it shows a young woman being decapitated."

"Special effects?" Jenny suggested.

"The girl in the picture is Bunny Miller," Jackson replied.

"Oh, shit," John said. "And you found that in Uncle Billy's car?"

"Yes. Well, we almost didn't find it. Evidently it was lying on the dashboard when the car went over the embankment. The impact of the crash at the bottom caused the car to twist. That must have opened up a gap at the front of the dashboard and the tape slipped down behind it. Every one of us missed it the first time, but when the car was brought into impound, one of the men there found it. They saw just the corner of the tape, sticking down from behind the dash."

"Uncle Billy wasn't into that kind of thing," John said. "This just doesn't seem like him."

"Maybe not," Jackson said. "But it was in his car."

"I thought you said the tape wasn't in the car," an accusatory voice from the other end of the phone line said.

"I didn't think it was. I searched as best I could last night, but it was dark and I didn't see it."

"It was dark," the voice scoffed. "It's dark every night."

"Even the cops didn't find it. Not until the car went to impound."

"Yeah, well, you find some way to get the tape back."

"How am I going to do that?"

"How the hell do I know? That's your job, not mine. Just do it. Get the tape back."

ELEVEN

John and Jenny listened to Don gag, heave, gag, then heave again. After that the toilet was flushed; then they heard water running in the lavatory. Don came back into the room, wiping his face with a damp washcloth. His face was so pale that it was nearly blue.

"Are you all right?" Jenny asked.

"Yeah." Don sat down on the couch and leaned his head back. For a long moment all three were silent; then Don pointed to the TV screen. The video they had just watched was still in the tape deck.

"You know, it's bad enough to watch that kind of shit when it isn't real," he said. "But when it is real it's . . ." He stopped in mid-sentence, unable to put his thought into words.

"I know what you mean," Jenny said. "It is just about the most awful thing I've ever seen."

"Listen, you don't think we are responsible for this, do you?" Don asked.

"What do you mean?" John asked.

"Well, this girl tried to help us and look what happened to her."

Jenny shook her head. "I don't even want to think that. Besides, she's not the only one helping us. I mean, someone left us the note about *Oval Orifice,* and it couldn't have been Bunny, because she was already dead when we got the note."

"So what is the significance of *Oval Orifice*, and who left it?" John asked.

"Someone who is trying to help us," Jenny answered.

"It would be a lot more help if whoever it was had left us their name."

"Can you blame them for their anonymity?" Don asked. "Bunny helped us, and look what happened to her."

"We don't know that," Jenny said. "On the other hand, I think this proves that she didn't set us up willingly."

"So, what do we do next, Boss?" Don asked.

"I think the next step is pretty obvious. We have to get our hands on a copy of *Oval Orifice.*"

"Oval Orifice?" Bo Peep replied when questioned about the videotape. She laughed. "Sure I've seen it. It's a hoot."

"A hoot?"

"Yes, it's funny," Bo Peep said.

"One doesn't often hear the word 'funny' applied to an erotic video," Jenny said.

"Well, now, see, that's just because you are prejudiced against the genre," Bo Peep said. "A lot of them are funny, and a lot of them are poignant. I know, there are the typical dirty mattress on the basement floor and handheld-camera videos, but there are also those with great stories and good production values."

"You make a good spokesperson for the industry," Don said.

Bo Peep beamed proudly. "I believe everyone should take pride in their work."

"Tell me, Bo Peep, you wouldn't happen to know where we could get a copy of *Oval Orifice*, would you?" John asked.

"Are you cops?"

"Cops? No, why do you ask? What would that have to do with it?"

"Well, do you remember the actress you showed me a picture of? The one I said that all the video was pulled because she was underage? Well, she is also the one who did *Oval Orifice*."

"So *Oval Orifice* has been pulled?"

Bo Peep looked around to make certain she wasn't overheard. "We did pull it," she said. "But the boss held a few copies back for some of his special customers. Come this way."

Bo Peep led them through an aisle, flanked on both sides with racks of videos, many of them proudly proclaiming to be the "Hottest Adult Erotica" ever filmed. Then, looking around to make certain she wasn't seen by the customers, she bent down below the racks, opened a door, then reached in the back and pulled out a cassette.

"Here it is," she said, handing the tape to him.

In the background was a picture of the White House. In the foreground, the Oval Office, with the Presidential Seal prominently displayed. A tall man with silver hair, looking suspiciously like the President, was leaning back against his desk. One hand was holding a telephone to his ear while the other hand was on the back of a young girl's head. The young girl, wearing a blue dress and black beret, was on her knees, performing oral sex.

"We'd like to rent this," John said.

* * *

Back in the motel the three watched the video. It had a simple plotline. Annette was an intern who was infatuated with the President. She wanted to get into the Oval Office to see him, but she was stymied at every turn by White House guards, Secret Service operatives, and White House staffers. In order to get by them she had to engage in various kinds of sex with them, including one scene in which she performed cunnilingus on the President's blond-haired, shrewlike wife.

In the final scene she was shown performing fellatio on the President while he was ordering a series of air attacks against small countries overseas. The film ended with a slow-motion close-up of Presidential ejaculum splashing onto her blue dress.

"Well," Jenny said as the screen went black, "the picture is in incredibly bad taste, it is probably libelous, though safe because no one would want to call attention to something like that, and it is poorly written. At least it isn't S&M."

"That's true," John agreed. "Unless one takes into consideration that the viewer is in pain while watching it."

"I, on the other hand, give it a clear thumbs-up," Don said. "I found the production value stunning, the performances riveting, and the story poignant and well conceived."

John and Jenny looked at Don for a second in total shock, then, realizing that he was spoofing them, they both laughed.

"This turned out to be a dead end," Jenny said. "So what do we do now?"

"I think I'll pay Wet Spot Productions another visit," John said. "Don, you get back on the computer, peruse the Internet, and see what you can find. Jenny?"

"I know, I know," Jenny said. "You want me to start peddling my ass again."

"No, I want you to advertise it," John said. "Not sell it."

"Where's the fun in all show and no go?" Jenny teased.

When Jenny returned to the streets, she was warmly greeted by Sheeba. A few of the others looked at her suspiciously, and one of them asked where she had been.

"What do you mean?" Jenny asked.

"Well, here's the thing, girl," she was told. "When someone just shows up now and again, then she leaves for a long time, then she comes back, well, it makes a person suspicious, you know what I mean? For all we know you could be some kind of undercover cop, comin' out here to try and bust our ass."

"René, don't pay any attention to Dawn," Sheeba said to Jenny, using Jenny's street name. "Dawn's just jealous because you got that trip with a rich john. Five thousand dollars and all you had to do was spend a week on a boat."

"What you talkin' about?" Dawn asked.

Sheeba winked at Jenny as if saying, "Play along with me on this," then looked at the others. "Some rich man gave her to his son for a birthday present," she said.

"Wow, what a gig that would be!" one of the other girls said.

"How did it go, René? Did you break that young

boy in?" Sheeba asked. Sheeba was clearly having fun with her story now.

"It was fine," Jenny said, getting into the act as well. "Being as the boy was a virgin, he didn't have any experience, but he did have quite a sexual appetite. But I've always had a bit of the school teacher in me. I enjoyed providing the lessons."

"Man, you talk about someone lucky," one of the other girls said. "Here you been in the life no more than a few weeks, and you land a gig like that."

"You mean you don't get this kind of job very often?" Jenny asked innocently.

"Honey, that's the kind of thing every girl in the life dreams of. But you're the first one I've ever seen it actually happen to."

Sheeba's explanation as to Jenny's whereabouts over the last few days seemed to satisfy everyone, and the curious questions stopped. As the johns began cruising, the other girls began to make connections until, once again, Jenny found herself alone with Sheeba.

"Thanks, Sheeba," Jenny said. She chuckled. "That was quite some story you made up."

"Yes, well, like Dawn said, we sometimes fantasize about things like that. I figured if I was going to make up a story about you, I'd make up a good one. Besides, I was having fun with it."

Jenny laughed. "I think we all were," she said. She grew more serious. "Have you had anymore trouble with Downtown?"

Sheeba laughed out loud. "You mean Uptown?" she said. "No, I haven't had any more trouble with him. Last time I saw him he had this big-assed scab on his nose where you pulled out the nose ring." She laughed again. "I tell you the truth, girl, even if he had come back and given me an ass-whipping, it would've been worth it."

"He had better not come back on you," Jenny said. "If he does, I'll make him wish he hadn't."

"You're just the girl that can do it too," Sheeba said. "Oh, by the way, did you get the note I left you?"

"Oval Orifice? That was you?"

"Yes. Since Tulip was in it, I thought you might be interested."

"I was, thanks."

"I guess she got what she wanted," Sheeba said. "But, like I told you, I may want to give up the life some day and marry an accountant. And if I do, I wouldn't want anything like that to come back and bite me in the ass."

"I don't blame you," Jenny said. "Tell me, Sheeba, have you ever heard of snuff films?"

The smile left Sheeba's face and she shivered. "Girl, what are you asking about something like that for?"

"Then you know what they are?"

"Yes, I know what they are. Do you?"

"Unfortunately, I do know. I watched one this morning."

"You watched one of those things?" Sheeba asked, shocked by the revelation. "Why would you want to see one?"

"Believe me, I didn't want to see it."

"Do you think it was real?"

Jenny was silent for a moment; then when she spoke, her words were so low that Sheeba had to strain to hear them. "It was real, all right. Sheeba, the girl in the film was Bunny."

"Bunny? In a snuff film? No, she would never

do anything like that. I mean, stand by and watch while some poor girl gets whacked? Not Bunny."

"You don't understand," Jenny said. "Bunny didn't stand by and watch someone else get whacked. Bunny was the one who got whacked."

Sheeba gasped. "What?" she asked in a weak voice.

"Bunny is dead."

Sheeba shook her head and held up her hands. "No," she said in a weak voice. She backed away from Jenny as if, by separating herself from the messenger, she could distance herself from the message. "You just think she is. There are so many special effects now, and these geeks who work with computers can make anything look real." Sheeba tried to force a laugh. "That—that's all it was. You just got fooled by it, that's all."

"No. I wish you were right, but Bunny really is dead," Jenny said. "I not only saw the film, I saw her body."

Tears sprang to Sheeba's eyes and, quickly, she walked several feet away to stand near the brick wall of the closest building. Putting her hand on the wall, she leaned against it, standing there for a long moment.

"I'm sorry, Sheeba."

Sheeba tried to say something, but no words came out. She shook her head and choked back a sob as tears slid down her cheeks. Jenny gave her some time to compose herself. Finally, Sheeba turned back toward Jenny and wiped her eyes. "Bunny and I talked about X-rated movies," she said. "From time to time people would come around, 'recruiting talent,' they said. Every time they did that, quite a few of the girls would go along with them. But Bunny was like I am. She didn't want anything like that in her past either."

"I don't think she was in this picture by choice," Jenny said. "She was tied up, and she looked like she was doped up."

Sheeba shook her head. "No, that can't be right. Bunny didn't do dope. Why, I bet she never even smoked more than half-a-dozen marijuana cigarettes. If she was doped up, they did it to her."

"What do you mean, they? Who are they?"

"They," Sheeba said. "The people who made the picture."

"Do you have any idea who that might be?"

"No."

"Think hard."

"I don't know anyone who would make such a film," Sheeba said. "And if I did know them, I wouldn't want to have anything to do with them. What's all this got to do with what you're out here investigating?"

"Nothing, I hope," Jenny said. "I'm still operating under the premise that Annette, or Tulip as she called herself, is just a teenage runaway. And I hope that's all there is to it. But I have to examine all possibilities."

John took a copy of *Oval Orifice* with him when he returned to Wet Spot Productions. As soon as he stepped into the lobby, Wanda greeted him as if he were an old friend.

"Mr. Todaro," she said, flashing him a broad smile. "How nice to see you again. Are you enjoying your visit to Los Angeles?"

"Yes," John said. "It has been most productive."

"Just a moment, I'll let Mr. Sarducci know you

are here," Wanda said. She punched a number, then said, "Mr. Sarducci, you wanted me to let you know the moment Mr. Todaro returned? He's here now."

As Wanda hung up the phone, she happened to glance at the videotape John was carrying. "Oh, I see you have a copy of *Oval Orifice*. Wasn't Tulip wonderful in that picture?"

John was somewhat taken aback by Wanda's comment. It was as casual as if two people at a cocktail party were discussing a favorite film. Only this wasn't a normal film, this was an X-rated, very graphic video. In addition, the star of the film was underage.

"You know this picture?" John asked.

"Of course I know it. It is—that is, it was—one of our most popular pictures."

"Was?"

"Yes. We had to recall it, you know. Turns out the young lady star was underage, though of course we didn't know it at the time. It's a shame about her, you know. She had such potential. I believe she was true star quality. Such a lovely young thing."

"But she was underage?"

"Yes, but not by more than a few months. Of course, Mr. Sarducci knew nothing about it. She swore that she was over eighteen, and she had a California driver's license to prove it."

"How did you find out she wasn't eighteen?"

"Oh, I believe it was Sergeant Wallace of the LAPD who told us."

"Sergeant Wallace told you? Are you sure it was Sergeant Wallace?"

"Oh, yes, he is in charge of Vice, I believe, so he is a frequent visitor. We count on him to keep us all legal and aboveboard," Wanda said.

The door into the back opened, and Tony Sarducci came breezing through.

"Mr. Todaro," he said, his hand extended and a smile plastered on his face. "How good of you to come back!"

John was glad Sarducci came out to see him, but he cursed the timing. He would have liked to talk to Wanda for a few minutes longer.

"Listen, you are just in time," Sarducci said. "We are shooting a scene back in the studio right now. Would you care to watch?"

"Well, I—"

"I think you will enjoy it. It features Amber La-Mour. Amber is a beautiful woman and is one of the true stars in the adult film industry. I'm sure she will keep you interested."

The last thing John wanted to do was watch a porn film being made, and he almost declined. Then he realized that this would give him an excellent opportunity to have a closer look at the studio.

"Well, now, who wouldn't take advantage of an opportunity like this?" he asked. "I just don't want to be an intrusion."

"No intrusion. After all, you are part of our business. We'll just call this a professional consultation."

TWELVE

The studio was a cavernous room with very high ceilings, scores of light tracks, towering stands, cameras, monitors, sound equipment, and piles of flats. "So, what do you think of the operation?" Sarducci asked, taking in the studio with a sweep of his hand.

"Very impressive."

"It should be. It's state-of-the-art, digital." He became pensive. "And I'm wasting it all on porn."

"I beg your pardon?" John asked, surprised by the comment.

"Nothing," Sarducci said. "Forget I said anything. You know, I almost had a network contract for my TV show *Beach Vice*, but the smarmy bastards squirmed out of it at the last minute." Sarducci chuckled. "So, I got into the adult entertainment business."

"And you don't like the adult entertainment business?"

"Artistically, I hate it. But I must confess that, business-wise, it is the best thing I've ever done. Did you know that making adult videos is the most lucrative genre in the business? On a cost-and-return basis, that is. We beat the more traditional film industry five to one."

"I can see the attraction," John said.

The studio was in heavy shadow except for a spill of light in one corner. John looked toward the light, but several cameras, a bank of monitors, and switching equipment blocked his view. He shivered, then realized that it was cold in there, so cold that he could see his breath.

"Damn," he said. "Do you hang meat in here?"

"What?"

"It's cold in here."

"Oh, yeah, hang meat. Ha, that's funny. Hell, you're in the business. You mean you've never been in a studio before?"

"Not one like this."

"Well, when all those lights go on, believe me, it gets plenty hot in here. So we have to keep it really cold to start with; otherwise the air conditioners would never be able to overtake the heat."

They moved toward the bright corner. There, a set was made up to resemble a bedroom. An almost-studious-looking young woman, with horn-rimmed glasses and blond hair pulled back into a bun, was sitting on the edge of the bed reading a paperback novel. She was bundled up in a heavy flannel robe, and so involved in the novel that she seemed totally oblivious to all the activity that was going on around her. Lighting technicians were taking readings, cameramen were adjusting cameras, and sound people were testing microphones.

"That's Amber LaMour," Sarducci said, pointing to the woman.

One of the technicians said something to her and, casually, but without looking up from her book, Amber let one side of her robe fall down. By that action she exposed her left shoulder and breast. The technician put a light meter on her skin, at the shoulder, on the breast, and even on the nipple. All the while, he was talking into a mike and headset, though his words were so quiet that no one but the person at the other end of the headset could hear what he was saying. When he was finished, Amber pulled the robe back up.

"That's Mr. Rand," Sarducci said, pointing to a short, fat man. "He's one of the best directors in this genre."

"Rock?" Rand called. "Rock, are you here?"

"I'm over here," a young man answered. He had been sitting in a chair to one side of the set. Like Amber, he was wearing a heavy flannel robe.

"That's Rock Hardon," Sarducci said.

"Hard-on?"

"Well, it's supposed to look like that when the credits roll across the screen. But he pronounces it Harden."

"Are you ready, Rock?" Rand asked.

"Just about."

"Take off your robe."

Rock dropped his robe. He had a magnificent build, and was obviously well suited for the role, though, at the moment, he was flaccid.

"Damn, you aren't ready. You don't even have a hard-on."

"Don't worry about me. I'll get it up. I always do."

"Now, Rock," Rand said insistently. "I want it up now. When you come into the picture, I want that thing standing out like a sword."

Sarducci chuckled. "Rand is good, isn't he? He gets the most out of these people."

"How do you know she's ready?" Rock complained, pointing to Amber. "For all you know, she might be dry as a bone. You never say anything to her."

"I'm always ready," Amber said, holding up a tube of lubricant jelly.

"Bitch," Rock said.

"Bitch," Amber replied.

"Bruce, help Rock get ready," Rand ordered, and a young, effeminate man went over to sit beside the star. He put his hand down between Rock's legs.

"What the hell?" John asked.

Sarducci chuckled. "The magic of show business. Things aren't always what they seem."

A bell rang, and Amber made an amazing transformation. Her glasses came off, and she let her hair down, then took off her robe. From what could have been a college student studying for an exam, she morphed into a beautiful, sensual creature, positively exuding pheromones.

When Rock, now fully erect, approached the bed, Amber looked at him with a face that was flushed with desire. Given the way they had spoken to each other earlier, John was ready to concede that, despite the type of picture they were in, they really could act.

While the couple writhed on the bed, and the cameramen moved in and out for various angles, John looked around the studio. He was trying to find something that he might recognize from the snuff film, but everything looked different.

"It's different, isn't it?" Sarducci said.

"What?" John asked in surprise.

"I see that you are having a hard time watching them. There is a big difference between watching people do this on film, and watching them do it in person."

"Oh. Yes, it is different."

"Wanda can't watch it," Sarducci said about the woman in front. "She can watch the films like a trooper, but try and get her in here to watch a live performance, and she turns to melted butter."

"I guess some of us are just that way," John said.

"Yes, well, I must confess that even I had a hard time getting used to it," Sarducci said. "Like I told you, I would much rather be making more traditional pictures, but"—he sighed—"it was either this or lose my studio. And I will do whatever it takes to hang on to the studio."

"The money shot, the money shot, Rock!" Rand suddenly shouted. "Give me the money shot!"

"Oh, oh, oh!" Rock started shouting.

"Yes, yes, yes!" Amber screamed.

John concentrated his gaze on the stack of flats that was lying alongside the wall near his chair. This was not something he cared to watch.

Midnight,
Sunset Boulevard,
Hollywood

A silver BMW stopped at the curb and the right window slid down. Smiling seductively, Sheeba stepped toward the curb. She leaned down so she could look in through the window. "This is a mighty fine-looking car you have," she said.

"I like it," the driver replied. The driver was wearing boots, jeans, an orange button-down shirt, and a cowboy hat.

"Honey, you look just like my prom date back home in Missouri," Sheeba said. "Boots, jeans, and hat. The only difference is, he was driving a pickup truck."

"Did you show your prom date a good time?" the driver asked.

Sheeba thrust her hip to one side. "Darlin', I showed that boy the best time he ever had."

"How 'bout showin' me a good time?"

"Well, I'm willing to do that, sugar, but you have to understand, you aren't my prom date. I'm a professional girl now."

The driver stuck his hand down in his jeans pocket and pulled out a large roll of cash. "Whatever it takes," he said. He leaned over and opened the door, inviting her in.

"Then what do you say we go find someplace to party?" Sheeba suggested as she got into the car.

As soon as the door was shut, the driver pulled away from the curb. "My name is Sheeba," she said. "What's yours?"

The driver didn't answer.

"That's okay, honey, I didn't expect you to tell me your real name. I'll just call you Cowboy."

Cowboy didn't answer.

"You wouldn't be from Texas, would you?" Sheeba asked.

Cowboy still didn't answer.

"That's all right, I don't really want to know," Sheeba said. "This way I can pretend you are from home."

Sheeba looked out the window. "Back in Missouri, I was Miss Blodgett, did you know that? Yes, sir, you are looking at a genuine beauty queen. When I got on the bus, some of my friends saw me off. They held up signs saying that I was Blodgett's gift to Hollywood." Sheeba was quiet for a long moment. "I wonder what they would think of me now?"

Cowboy turned onto Mulholland Drive, then started climbing up into the hills.

"What are you coming up here for?" Sheeba asked. "Wait a minute, you aren't planning on going parking, are you?" She laughed. "This is too much, we're going to screw in your car?"

"Why not?" Cowboy replied.

"Damn, you can talk."

"You said I reminded you of your prom date. Didn't you and your prom date do it in the truck?"

"No, on prom night he had his dad's Buick, and we did it in the backseat," Sheeba said. "But I was eighteen then. I've been rode hard and put away wet too many times since then. If you want this girl, you're going to have to find a room somewhere. Honey, I'm not doin' it in a car."

"Don't worry," Cowboy said. "I was just teasing you about doing it in the car. We're going to a party."

"A party? What kind of party?"

"A friend of mine owns a house up here. He's invited us up."

"You have a friend who owns a house in Beverly Hills? He must be a rich friend."

"He is," Cowboy said.

"Wait a minute, what do you mean he's invited us? He doesn't even know about me."

"Yes, he does," Cowboy said. "He sent me out to get you. He's very shy."

"He sent you to find me?"

"Well, maybe not you in particular. What he said was, 'I would like to have a good-looking woman tonight. Will you go find one for me?' You were the best-looking one I saw."

"Do you always find his women for him?"

"I have to. Otherwise the little shit would never get laid."

Sheeba laughed. "Does he know that I'm a, uh, that you were going to get a . . . ?"

"Whore? Oh, yes, he knows," Cowboy said. "He likes whores. He says there is no nonsense about them. It's a simple business proposition. He has the money and you have the product."

"Your friend sounds like a very practical person," Sheeba said.

"Oh, he is." Cowboy stopped at a gated driveway. "Well, this is it," he said. "We can either go on in, or I'll give you fifty dollars for your trouble and take you back. It's up to you."

"Are you kidding? I've come this far. Let's go on in."

Cowboy took a remote from behind one of the sun visors and pointed it at the gate. The gate swung open and they drove through.

The driveway was at least a quarter of a mile long. It passed over a little stream, by a stand of trees, through a natural garden, then around a fountain to stop in front of the house, a large, architectural experiment in planes and angles. Behind the house, which was dark, and down in the valley, the lights of Los Angeles twinkled brightly.

"What do you think?" Cowboy asked.

"It's beautiful, but also sort of overwhelming," Sheeba said.

"I thought you'd like it." Cowboy leaned across her and opened the door. "Well, get out."

"Get out? You mean, just like that? You aren't coming with me?"

"I told you, you're his whore, not mine," Cowboy said.

"But aren't you going to at least introduce us? I mean, I don't even know who he is, or what he looks like."

"What the hell difference does that make?" Cowboy asked. "This isn't a social encounter, this is a business proposition. Hell, how many different men are you with every night? Just go on up there and ring the doorbell."

"But there are no lights on. I don't even know if he is here."

"He's here. The house is so big that you can have half the lights on inside, and nobody outside would even know."

Hesitantly, and feeling increasingly uneasy about the whole thing, Sheeba slid slightly toward the door, but before she got out she looked back at Cowboy.

"Now what?" Cowboy asked irritably.

"You know what? I've changed my mind. I think I would rather take that fifty dollars you mentioned and go on back to town."

Cowboy shook his head. "It's too late now. You've already come onto the grounds. That offer was made on the other side of the gate, if you remember. Now, go on. Get out of the car and go up to the door like I told you to."

Sheeba climbed out of the car. She took a couple of steps toward the house, straining to see if there really were any lights on anywhere. The nameless sense of dread she had been feeling ever since Cowboy told her she would have to face the man alone overpowered her. She turned back toward the car, determined that she was going to return to town. But it was too late, because even as she was turning around, Cowboy drove off.

"Wait!" Sheeba called, and she ran several steps after him until it was obvious that he wasn't going to stop.

Breathing hard from her exertion, Sheeba stood

there for a long moment, then, fighting to over-
come the apprehension, turned back toward the
house. If her phantom date was here, she would
face up to him. She had no other choice now.

As Sheeba walked up the drive toward the house,
she heard a low, beastly growling. And if one growl
wasn't frightening enough, she heard two growls,
overlaid on each other. The hackles on the back
of her neck stood up and she felt a weakness in
her knees and in the pit of her stomach. Turning
toward the trees to her right, she saw two sets of
yellow eyes, glowing at her from the dark.

"Oh, my God!" she yelled. She started toward
the front of the building. "Help! Please, help! Let
me in!"

Hollywood Police Station

"Her real name was Norma Jean Collier," Lieutenant Jackson said.

"Yes, she told me that much," Jenny replied.
"Also that she was from a little place in Missouri."

"Her father is a farmer and her mother a school-
teacher. She has one brother in the Army and a
sister attending school at Southeast Missouri State
University."

Jackson handed Jenny a photograph of the girl.
She had large eyes, naturally heavy eyelashes, and
a large, innocent smile. "She was a beauty queen.
Like hundreds of other beauty queens come to
Hollywood to make their mark."

Only by concentrating hard could Jenny make
the connection between this picture of a girl-next-
door and the person she knew as Sheeba.

"Damn," Jenny said. She handed the picture to

John. Don moved over to examine it as well. "What happened to her?" Jenny asked.

"You aren't going to believe this," Jackson said. "She was attacked by cougars."

"Cougars? In downtown Hollywood?"

Jackson shook his head. "She was in Beverly Hills, on the George Gibson estate."

"Beverly Hills? That was a little out of her territory, wasn't it?" Jenny asked. "And who is George Gibson?"

"He's a well-known animal wrangler for the movie industry," Jackson said. "Anytime you see animals in a movie, lions, bears, wolves, whatever, the chances are pretty good that Gibson supplied them. He has a special license to raise wild animals, and he keeps them on a fifty-acre ranch up in Beverly Hills."

"Like I said, that was a little out of Sheeba's territory. What was she doing up there?" Jenny said.

"Hell, I can tell you that. She was peddling her ass," Sergeant Wallace said, coming over to join them. "I think she got tired of the creeps and perverts who cruise the streets at night, and decided to do a little market exploration," Wallace said. "She didn't pay any attention to all the 'keep out' and 'private property' signs, so she winds up getting mauled by a couple of cougars."

"What does Gibson have to say about this?" John asked.

"Nothing," Wallace said. "Turns out he wasn't even there. He was over in Africa. We're trying to get hold of him now, but he's out in the bush somewhere."

"And he just lets his animals wander around his estate while he's gone?" Jenny asked.

"No, not normally. He has a gamekeeper," Jackson said. "The gamekeeper swears that all the animals were safely secured when he left the property yesterday, and there are two people who back him up on it. But somehow, those two cougars got out of their containment and were wandering around on the grounds when Miss Collier happened onto the property."

"You know, what puzzles me is why the cougars attacked her in the first place," John said. "I mean, if they were movie animals, wouldn't you think they would be acclimated to humans? At least to the point to where they wouldn't attack them?"

"I wondered about that too," Jackson said, "and I asked the gamekeeper. He said these two were Gibson's latest acquisitions and they had a history of being temperamental. In fact, one of them attacked him just a week ago. He said if they weren't able to get them calm soon, they were going to have to let them back out into the wild."

"Where are the animals now?" John asked.

"They've been destroyed, both of them," Jackson said.

"Too bad," Wallace put in. "They shouldn't have killed them. They should've given them both a medal for service to the community."

"You are a man of great compassion, Sergeant Wallace," John said sarcastically.

"I have no sympathy for whores," Wallace said. "They are a chancre on the community. That's why I cut them no slack."

"As you can see, Sergeant Wallace is a man who is particularly motivated in the performance of his duties," Jackson said.

"You're damn right," Wallace said. "Three dead whores so far this month. If we keep that up, we'll have the city cleaned out in no time."

Two days later,
four P.M.,
Middle-class residential area,
Los Angeles

With his arms folded across his chest, Doc leaned back against the side of the blue Ford van and watched a young girl ride by on a bicycle. He could not see a young girl on a bicycle without thinking of Tamara. It had been twenty-eight years since his daughter was killed, hit by a drunk driver while she was riding home from school.

Doc's own life had unwound since then. In succession he became an alcoholic, then lost his position at St. Luke's Hospital, then lost his license to practice medicine. His marriage broke up and he dropped out of the society that he knew. Since that time he had not been in contact with any family member or acquaintance from his "other" life. Most of his old relatives and acquaintances thought he was dead.

Tamara would have been forty this year. There was no doubt she would have been married, with children, maybe even a little girl like the young girl on the bicycle.

Doc shook his head to clear his mind of such thoughts. He didn't often dwell on what might have been. It was hard enough to keep up with what was.

He and Kate were not married, but they had lived together for nearly ten years. They met in a bar. Kate was a former prostitute who had served time in prison for killing her pimp. The jury didn't buy her plea of self-defense, but everyone agreed that the pimp needed killing, so she was convicted of manslaughter and served less than three years.

They began by sharing drinks, then hard-luck

stories, then their lives. They opened an adult book and video store, but the competition was so fierce that they barely made a living. Then they discovered a segment of the business that proved to be extremely profitable.

Both Doc and Kate justified their participation in the child-pornography business by drawing a line they would not cross. That line was sixteen.

"Hell, forty percent of all kids are sexually active by the time they are sixteen," Doc liked to say.

"I started at fourteen," Kate would add.

"I see no real crime in letting a few voyeurs watch kids do what they were going to do anyway."

Of course, they had no way of knowing how old the girls in their videos really were, but they reviewed every video and if they seemed younger than sixteen, they wouldn't handle them.

Then, last week, they came across a revised edition of *Oval Orifice*, a version with a very disquieting ending. Disturbed by it, Doc called his supplier.

"I don't know where this came from, and I hope it isn't real. But just to let you know how disturbed I was by this film, I'll tell you right now that if I ever get anything like this again, I will go to the police with it."

Doc's supplier assured him that he was overreacting. He reminded Doc that they had made a lot of money together and threatening to go to the police was no way to continue what had been, until now, a profitable relationship.

It had been very profitable for Doc and Kate, and they had managed to save a good deal of money. It was their plan to retire in one more year, and move to Hawaii.

Doc looked at his watch, then back toward the house. "Kate," he called. "Get a move on it."

Kate came out of the house, carrying a sack of videotapes. "I'm coming, I'm coming," she said. "I had to rewind some of these."

"You know how skittish our particular clients are," Doc said. "If we aren't at the meeting place at the exact time, they will walk away. And everyone who walks away costs us one hundred dollars."

"I still have to get the tapes in the pockets."

"Do that while we're driving," Doc said. "You know how bad the traffic is this time of day. We have to get started."

Doc slid the side door open and Kate climbed in, then opened the felt panel on the side. She was already sorting the tapes as Doc closed the door, then went around to his side.

"Are you strapped in?" Doc asked as he got behind the steering wheel.

"No."

"Why not?"

"You know I can't reach all the pockets if I'm strapped in."

"Well, get it done as quickly as you can, then buckle up. The way these people drive out here, you can't be too careful." Doc reached for the key.

Twelve-year-old Sandy didn't like the way the man back at the van had looked at her when she rode by, so she pedaled her bike just a little faster, opening up the distance between them. She had just reached the far end of the block when the pressure wave from the blast hit her. The wave was so strong that it almost knocked her over, and she had to fight to maintain control of the bike. Concurrent with the pressure wave was the sound. It was the loudest noise she had ever heard. Sandy stopped the bike, put her foot down on the ground, then looked behind her.

The van was on fire, so covered by flames and smoke that if she didn't know what color it was, she wouldn't be able to tell now by looking.

"Oh, my God! What was that?" a woman shouted, running out onto the front porch of her house. All up and down the street, people were running out into their front yards to see what had happened. A thick, oily smoke roiled up from the van, twisting into a black column that rose high into the sky.

Sandy looked for the man who had been leaning against the van, but she didn't see him. She wondered if he had been hurt, or maybe even killed. The thought frightened and distressed her, so she got back on her bike and rode away as fast as she could.

Sergeant Larry Wallace was the first police officer on the scene, arriving even before the fire truck or ambulance. With his portable fire extinguisher in hand, he jumped out of the car and moved quickly toward the blazing inferno.

"Get back!" he called, waving his hand at the gathering crowd, while at the same time displaying his badge. "Get back, all of you!"

Wallace tried to get close enough to the van to use his extinguisher, but the heat was too great. It was a losing battle anyway; his little bottle of CO_2 could do nothing against a fire this large. He was well aware of that before he even got out of his car, but he didn't want anyone to be able to say that he didn't try.

THIRTEEN

Over the Rocky Mountains,
Flight Level Forty-two

Less than one inch away from John's face, on the other side of the reinforced glass window, the temperature was sixty degrees below zero and the oxygen level was as thin as it is on the surface of the planet Mars. Inside, the cabin was pressurized to a very breathable eight thousand feet, and the temperature was a comfortable seventy-two degrees. There was only a whisper of the jet-engine noise and a six-hundred-mile-per-hour wind stream to give any indication of the harshness outside.

John sank deep into the soft leather seat, which was much more like a lounge chair than an airline seat. In fact, it *was* a lounge chair, with the capability of tipping all the way back. And if that wasn't comfortable enough, there were four bunks in the back of the cabin.

The airplane was a Gulfstream IV, configured to provide the maximum comfort for the elite few who were lucky enough to be passengers. Through the window, John could look down onto America's roof, where snowcapped peaks gleamed gold in the setting sun. They were flying at Flight Level Forty-two, or forty-two thousand feet. Up here, the ride was as smooth as if they were in a well-sprung car gliding across a superhighway. Had they been lower, they would be experiencing the turbulence created by wind shears as the tide of air rolled across the Rocky Mountain range.

This airplane was one of a fleet of such airplanes belonging to Marist Quinncannon. It was operated by a crew of four consisting of pilot, copilot, flight attendant, and chef. In its current configuration it could carry fourteen, though John, Jenny, and Don were the only passengers aboard. The crew, as was their custom, treated any passenger on this airplane as if they were royalty.

The chef approached Jenny. "Madam," he said in one of those cultured accents that, like the faux accents adopted by the National Public Radio announcers on the classical-music programs, couldn't quite be placed. "For dinner you have a choice of broiled steak and lobster, broiled tomatoes, dilled zucchini, noodles with poppy seed, and endive salad. Or, you may choose vichyssoise, fruited chicken en crème, and green beans amandine."

"I'll take the fruited chicken," Jenny said.

"Very good, madam," the chef said. He turned to John. "And you, sir?"

"The steak and lobster sound good to me," John said.

Don was sitting behind Jenny, looking through the window. Earlier, he had asked the flight attendant if there was anything to eat, and she had brought him a little platter of brioches, butter, and orange marmalade.

"And you, sir. I know you had a little repast a short while ago. Will you still be wanting dinner?"

John and Jenny both laughed.

"You may as well ask a man dying of thirst in the desert if he wants water," John suggested.

"Or a dog if he wants a bone," Jenny added.

"Pay no attention to them," Don said. "They are uncouth heathens, totally without social graces. I will be dining, thank you."

"Very good, sir. Steak and lobster, or fruited chicken?"

"Yes."

"I beg your pardon?"

"Yes," Don said again. "I'll have steak, lobster, fruited chicken, noodles, rice, green beans, all of it."

The chef blinked in surprise. "All of it, sir?"

"Yes. If that's possible," Don added.

"Oh, yes, sir, it is quite possible from my perspective," the chef said. "I'm just wondering about your capacity to, uh, assimilate such an order."

John and Jenny laughed again.

"Don't worry about Don's 'capacity to assimilate,' " Jenny said. "The man is a bottomless pit."

"Listen," Don said to Jenny. "Do you remember when you were a kid and your mother made you clean your plate by telling you about the starving children in China?"

Jenny shook her head. "No," she replied.

"Really? Well, I know that mothers all across the country did say that. And being Chinese, of course, I always felt a particular obligation to carry that out."

"Very good, sir," the chef said. "I will roll up my sleeves and get right to work." Hitching up his trousers, the chef gave a very good imitation of John Wayne. "I've a man's work to do this night."

All three laughed as the chef returned to the galley.

"Why do you think Mr. Quinncannon wanted us to come back to New York?" Jenny asked.

"I don't know. He said he'd rather not talk about it over the phone," John replied. "That's why he asked us to come see him."

"Well, I'll say this," Jenny said as she ran her hand along the burl-wood trim. "He certainly knows how to send for someone. I don't know that I've ever traveled quite so elegantly."

"I only wish we had something more to tell him," John said.

"Did you bring the tape of *Oval Orifice?*" Jenny asked.

"Yes, but I don't know if I want to show it to him."

"I don't blame you. Until we have something more definite, I see no reason to upset him by having him watch such a film."

"Oh, shit," Don suddenly said. He had his laptop computer set up and was studying the screen.

"What is it?" John asked.

"I'm looking at today's addition of the *Los Angeles Times.* You remember Doc and Kate?"

"Who?"

"The two people in the blue Ford Van? You know, the ones I got the tape from? They were Doc and Kate."

"Yes, I remember," John said.

"Hmm, turns out he really was a doctor," Don said, reading the article. "He was a gynecologist, though he had lost his license to practice. Their real names were Doctor Paul Brewer and Catherine Moss."

"Their real names *were?*"

"Yes," Don said. "They were both killed when a bomb was placed in their van. Police are theorizing that some anti-porn activist did it."

"You know what, guys?" Jenny said. "I'm beginning to have a really strange feeling about all this."

"So am I," John said. He counted off on his fingers. "Bunny helped us, she's dead. Uncle Billy helped us, he is dead. Sheeba helped us, and she is dead."

"Yeah, well, Doc and Kate didn't really help us," Don suggested.

"Oh, yes, they helped us, all right," John said. "They just didn't know they were helping us."

"At this point, it would be hard to connect them all, though," Jenny reminded them. "Bunny was murdered. We know that because we saw it on film. Uncle Billy was shot, but he associated with some pretty low-life characters. To suggest that his murder had anything to do with our investigation would be strictly hypothetical. And cougars killed Sheeba. You have to admit that, as a murder weapon, cougars aren't the most efficient thing you could use."

"Maybe not. On the other hand, cougar attacks don't leave powder residue on the shooter's hands," John said.

"I see what you mean," Jenny said. "It's hard to trace a cougar attack back to a specific individual."

"And Doc and Kate may really have been killed by an anti-porn crusader," Don said. "Some of those reform zealots get really psyched."

"True," John said. "Still, we can't avoid the fact that all of these people are connected with us."

"Well, yes," Don said. "But when you examine it more closely, you realize they aren't really connected to us. They are players in the world we are investigating, that's all. Why, you may as well say Lieutenant Jackson or Sergeant Wallace is responsible."

"Damn," John said.

"What?" Jenny asked. "You've had a thought."

"Didn't Wallace say that he had never seen Annette?"

"Yes, but we know he did, because she was arrested for unauthorized occupancy," Jenny replied.

"That doesn't really prove anything," Don said. "I'm sure young women come through the Hollywood Station every day. That doesn't mean they make an impression on anyone."

"Well, Annette must have made some kind of impression," John said. "Because Sergeant Wallace is the one who told Sarducci he would have to pull *Oval Orifice* from the market because she was underage. How could he possibly know that, unless he knew her?"

"Hmm, good question."

"You know, now that I think about it, there is something else Sergeant Wallace did that gives one pause for thought," Jenny said.

"What's that?"

"After Sheeba was killed he said, and I quote, 'Three dead whores so far this month. If we keep that up, we'll have the city cleaned out in no time.'"

"So?" Don said.

"Where did he come up with three?" Jenny asked. "Bunny is one, Sheeba is two, who is the third one? Does he mean Annette?"

"Not unless he knows something we don't know," John said.

At that moment the chef rolled a cart down the aisle. There were four meals on the cart, one each for John and Jenny, and two for Don. Even as the chef was serving Jenny, Don was reaching for one of his plates.

"I can see now that we are going to have to discuss this later," John said. "I don't think Don can eat and think at the same time."

* * *

At that particular moment, in close proximity to the Gulfstream, a Delta 737 was flying in the same direction, en route nonstop from Los Angeles to New York. The copilot of the Delta jet looked up and saw the Gulfstream. The business jet was ten thousand feet higher and fifty miles per hour faster than the airliner, and it passed them high overhead, slipping quickly through that cold, dark crystal air, leaving a long, golden contrail in its wake.

"Damn," the copilot said, pointing out the Gulfstream to his pilot. "Now that is the way to travel."

In that same Delta flight, the first-class passengers were being given their choice of grilled salmon or New York strip, while back in coach the passengers were choosing between a hamburger pasta and chicken and dressing.

In Seat 4a, Mehdi al Ahmed had just chosen the salmon. A young, pretty flight attendant leaned toward him.

"What would you like to drink?" she asked sweetly.

"I'll have coffee," Ahmed said.

"Very good, sir. And would you like me to put this in the overhead for you?" She reached for his canvas bag.

"No," Ahmed replied. He wrapped his arm around the canvas bag and pulled it closer to him. "I would like to keep it with me, if I may."

"Of course, if you prefer," she said.

As the attendant moved up the aisle, Ahmed paid particular attention to the curve and natural swing of her derriere. American women wore so few clothes that it took little imagination to mentally strip her. In his mind's eye he could see her skin, bare, white, and stained with a crimson streak of blood. The thought gave him an instant erection, and he moved the canvas bag over his lap to keep from embarrassing himself.

Ahmed had two videos in his canvas bag; one was labeled *Growing Wheat in America's Breadbasket*, the other *The Mississippi Delta, America's Rice Belt.*

"I'll bet this is some fascinating viewing," the security officer at LAX had said sarcastically when he had looked at the sleeve covers.

"I am taking them back to show to the school-children in my country," Mehdi Al Ahmed said. "We love America," he added.

"I'm sure you do," the security official said as he zipped the canvas bag shut.

Ahmed smiled as he thought of the stupid, naïve inspection. Neither of the videos had anything to do with agriculture. One was called *Rabbit Chop*, and the other was *Oval Orifice XSM.*

Ahmed was taking the tapes to Europe, where he would have them duplicated, then sold. Each copy would bring from one to five thousand dollars, depending on the area and market.

Of course, only the master tapes could be duplicated. Ahmed had developed a process whereby copies could not be recopied. That was absolutely necessary to protect the value of his investment.

Ahmed kept a very close inventory on the copies he made, limiting the reproduction so as to keep the price of each unit high. This time, though, he did something he had never done before. He gave one of the pictures away.

Giving the video away might have been bad from a business point of view, but in this case he was driven by something more than business. He was motivated by a twenty-year desire for revenge.

It wasn't merely a whim that led him to request a remake of the ending of *Oval Orifice*. He knew exactly what he was doing.

When the U.S. Government paid twenty million dollars to the "Party of God's Deprived" as reparations for what the current Administration called "the illegal attack against their religious sect by a private American citizen," it breathed new life into the moribund group. Their first act was to offer a one-million-dollar reward to anyone who would kill Marist Quinncannon. They also used the money to keep tabs on Quinncannon and his entire family. They knew, even before John, Jenny, Don, and the Los Angeles Police Department, that the underage girl in the adult video *Oval Orifice*, was Annette Quinncannon, Marist Quinncannon's granddaughter.

Because Mehdi al Ahmed's personal vendetta was all that remained of his once-religious fervor, he still had access to the information the Party of God's Deprived was able to glean. When he made a special request for a change in the ending of *Oval Orifice*, it provided a satisfying irony. And now, because of John Barrone's renewed association with Marist Quinncannon, his twenty-year mission was about to be brought to an exquisite conclusion.

Even'song Estate,
Long Island

"Vivian is visiting her parents," Marist Quinncannon said to John and the others. "Glen and Marie are gradually coming around to the idea that what Vivian and I feel for each other is genuine, despite the difference in our ages."

"I'm sure everything is going to work out all right between the two of you," Jenny said. "She seems like a very sensible, as well as beautiful, woman."

"Yes, I'm quite lucky to have her come into my life now," Quinncannon said. "Especially now, when we are sharing the pain of our mutual losses, first Jason, then Annette."

"I wish we had more information for you, Mr. Quinncannon, but—" John started. Quinncannon held out his hand to stop him.

"I may have some information for *you*. I chose this time to call you here because I knew Vivian would be away. I don't want her to see what I am about to show you. Indeed, I don't even want her to know that you came." Quinncannon walked over to his desk, opened a drawer, and took out a videotape cassette. He held the tape out, showing it to John and the others.

"This came in the mail. When I watched it, I was shocked and sickened. As you can imagine, I haven't shown it to Vivian. In fact, I will never show it to her, whether this proves to be real or not."

Quinncannon put the tape into the player, then turned it on. It opened with a picture of the White House, then the title: *Oval Orifice*.

John, Jenny, and Don cut a glance at each other, though they didn't let Quinncannon see their reaction.

"My first reaction was, is this my granddaughter?" Quinncannon said. "I know that may sound odd to you, but I am sure you can understand. At first glance, this person I am watching on the screen, doing all these unspeakable things, bears very little resemblance to my Annette. But upon closer examination, I am almost positive that it is."

John paused for a moment before he answered.

Then he took a deep breath, as if he were about to jump into a cold stream.

"Yes, sir. I believe it is Annette. We haven't been able to locate her yet, but we do know she took the name of Tulip, and we also know that she got involved with the adult film business."

"Adult film," Quinncannon said. "An interesting name for it, seeing as Annette is not yet an adult."

"True enough," John replied.

The images continued to flicker on screen.

"You weren't going to tell me about this?"

"No, sir, we weren't," John replied. "At least, not until we had more information. I didn't want to come to you with the job only half done."

Quinncannon was silent for a moment. "I can understand that," he finally said. He picked up the remote and pointed it toward the TV. John thought he was going to turn it off, having seen enough. To his surprise, however, Quinncannon clicked the fast-forward button. John watched the screen as Tulip went through a succession of sex partners in almost strobelike fashion: the gate guard, a couple of staff people, Secret Service people, the President's wife, and finally the President. John was trying to think of something to say to Quinncannon when he clicked it back to normal speed. This was the final scene, where Presidential ejaculum spurted onto Annette's dress.

John wondered why he slowed the film for this particular scene. Then all of a sudden he realized that the ending of this tape was going to be different from the one he had viewed.

"Oh, shit! A snuff!" Jenny gasped in quick surprise.

In this version, as the President finished ejaculating, he pulled a small pistol from his jacket pocket and put it to Annette's forehead. The expression on Annette's face was not the result of acting talent, but a true expression of fear and surprise. On screen, smoke billowed from the gun as it was fired. A small, black hole appeared in Annette's forehead as she was thrown back by the impact of the bullet. The film ended with a freeze-frame on her dead face. The picture went away and the words "The Final Solution" were superimposed over black.

Quinncannon turned off the tape, then looked at John. "As you can imagine, it was very difficult for me to watch my beautiful young granddaughter engaging in such debasing acts. But the most disturbing part of all is the violent ending. I know they can do amazing things with special effects now. Still . . ." He let the word hang.

Quinncannon waited for some sort of response from John or one of the others, but they remained quiet. When they didn't respond, the expression on Quinncannon's face changed from uneasiness to trepidation. He looked at Jenny.

"What did you mean when you said, 'Oh shit, a snuff'?"

Jenny turned to John, imploring him to answer for her.

"What is going on?" Quinncannon asked. He pointed to the blank screen. "Wait a minute! You aren't about to try and tell me that *is* real, are you? Did I just see a picture of my granddaughter being murdered?"

"I can't say for certain, Mr. Quinncannon," John finally said. "But, yes, I'm afraid that what you saw was real."

"Oh, my God!" Quinncannon said. Closing his eyes, he turned away from them, but not before they could see tears beginning to form.

"They are called snuff films," Jenny explained. "They are sexually explicit until the final scene. In the final scene someone is killed, or 'snuffed.' "

Quinncannon took a deep breath. When he opened his eyes again, they were red-rimmed and brimming with tears. "I don't understand," he said. "What kind of sick mind would conceive of such a thing? And why would they do it?"

"To answer your first question, Mr. Quinncannon, I don't think there is anything that is so depraved or so evil that someone, somewhere, won't do it," Don said. "And to answer your second question, there are people who are just as sick who will pay to see it. And they will pay well."

"When you say pay well, how much are you talking about?" Quinncannon asked.

"From what I have been able to find out, these tapes usually sell for from one to five thousand dollars a copy," Don said. "And worldwide they might sell as many as a thousand copies. That means the producer of this film will earn from one to five million dollars from an investment of only a few thousand."

"Five million? That is less than I make, just in interest, in a single day. So what you are saying is, some degenerate producer is willing to take the life of my beautiful granddaughter for what to me is pocket change. If I had known about this, I would have gladly paid that much and more to stop it. How long have you known about this?"

"Actually, we didn't know about this at all," John said. "We have seen this film before, but the version we saw didn't have this ending."

"Do you think there is a chance that she might still be alive?" Quinncannon asked hopefully.

John shook his head. "I'm sorry, Mr. Quinncannon. I don't want to give you any false hope by even suggesting that there is a possibility."

"I will have to tell Vivian." The sorrow in the old man's eyes was so boundless that it touched John at his core. Quinncannon closed his eyes and pinched the bridge of his nose for a long moment. When he opened them again, the sorrow had been replaced by a venomous loathing.

"Your mission has changed, Mr. Barrone," Quinncannon said. "I no longer want you to try and find my granddaughter. I know now that she is dead. What I want is for you to find the people who are responsible for this inhuman cruelty. I want you to find them and, to the degree that you are able, hold them accountable for their sins."

"Mr. Quinncannon, do you have any idea who sent you the tape?"

Quinncannon shook his head no.

"You don't have anyone else out there working this case, do you?"

Again, Quinncannon shook his head no.

"What I can't understand is why someone would send him this tape in the first place," Jenny said. "Who would want to hurt him that much?"

"Oh, my dear, I do have enemies," Quinncannon said. "As I am sure you perceived by the elaborate security system I have installed."

"Yes, I did notice the security system," Jenny said. "It seems effective."

"It is very effective. The only problem is that, it not only keeps the bad guys out, it keeps me in. I have become my own prisoner," he said.

FOURTEEN

It was easy for Ahmed to find four of his fellow countrymen who were willing to take part in the planned attack against John Barrone. Even though they were in the States on student visas, they continued to hold very strong anti-American feelings. Because they were young, they were still fired with the zeal to strike a blow for their people and to become martyrs for their religion. That ardor was strengthened even more when they were promised five thousand dollars apiece to help Ahmed kill John Barrone.

The helicopter pilot, Abdel Jahm Shedi, was a different story. He was not an idealist, having abandoned both his country and his religion. Jahm Shedi had been a pilot in the Royal Iranian Army, trained by the Americans before the overthrow of the Shah. After the revolution he left Iran and moved to the United States, but things did not go well for him here. Americans were unable, or unwilling, to distinguish between pro-American and anti-American Iranians. To Jahm Shedi's chagrin, he discovered that American prejudice knew no bounds; it was spread without discrimination to everyone with a Middle Eastern and/or Islamic background.

Jahm Shedi was not welcome in America and he could never return to Iran. He became a misanthrope who hated everyone, a man whose past was stolen and whose future was denied. He was a perfect recruit for Ahmed because the loyalty of such men, Ahmed had learned long ago, could be bought. It required only a high enough price to ensure fidelity. Ahmed was willing to pay that price.

From their orbiting position, high over Even'song Estate, Ahmed watched the car leave the compound, then start up Breeze Tree Road. He had already picked out a place where the road made a sharp turn through a thicket of trees. Cars entering that turn would not be able to see what was on the other side.

"We will wait for them there," he told Jahm Shedi, pointing to the curve in the road.

Jahm Shedi put the helicopter into a descent. The blades popped loudly, cavitating as they spiraled down through their own rotor wash. Ahmed sat in the open front door and armed the shoulder-held rocket launcher. The others took positions at the cargo door with their Uzis loaded and the safeties off.

Jahm Shedi terminated his descent, then held a hover inside the ground-effect bubble, about five feet above the surface of the road. Ahmed raised the sight on his rocket-launcher, aimed it toward the bend in the road where the car would appear, and waited.

"Open fire as soon as you see the car," he instructed the others.

The car came around the bend, heading straight for the hovering helicopter. The Uzis opened up, the sound of their firing audible above the noise of the helicopter. Ahmed pulled the trigger and watched as the rocket streamed into the car. The car erupted into a ball of fire, the hood flying upward, the doors tumbling out. The car left the road and plunged down an embankment into a ditch, where it burned fiercely.

"Ha!" Ahmed shouted. He pointed at the burning car. "I have waited twenty years for this, John Barrone!"

Suddenly the helicopter began to yaw wildly, climbing as it did so.

"What's happening?" Ahmed shouted in quick fear. They were now about twenty-five feet above the ground.

"Tail-rotor failure!" Jahm Shedi called back. "I can't hold it!"

As the helicopter spun around, Ahmed saw John Barrone standing in the middle of the road with his pistol in both hands, arms extended and locked, shooting up at them. Although Ahmed couldn't hear the shooting, he could see flashes of light coming from the barrel of Barrone's pistol. Because of the wild gyrations, no one in the helicopter could shoot back at him.

"He has shot out the tail rotor!" Jahm Shedi said.

"Where did he come from?" one of the others shouted. "How did he get out of the car?"

"He wasn't in the car!" Ahmed replied. "He tricked us!"

"Hold on! We are going down!" Jahm Shedi shouted.

Their descent from twenty-five feet was rapid and hard. When the helicopter hit the ground, the skids spread out and one of the rotor blades snapped off. The helicopter then began throwing pieces of aluminum and fiberglass, until finally everything came to a halt.

"Get out, quickly!" Jahm Shedi shouted. Even as he gave the order, he was unbuckling his own seat belt.

"Get out, get out!" Ahmed shouted to the young students in back. When he looked around to see if they heard him, he was horror-struck by what he saw. Half of one of the rotor blades had sliced down through the cabin to embed itself in the after bulkhead, just forward of the transmission deck. In order to get to that point, it had been necessary for the blade to pass through the four men in the back, decapitating them. Severed heads, blood, and brain matter filled the cabin.

For just a moment, Ahmed thought of the film *Rabbit Chop*, and he saw, not the four idealistic students, but the young black woman in the picture. He felt the bile of panic rising in his throat.

Had Allah sent him this vision?

"Get out, get out!" Jahm Shedi shouted again. "We've ruptured the fuel tanks. It's going to explode!"

Galvanized into action, Ahmed grabbed the little canvas bag that held his two snuff films and one of the Uzis. Then, jumping out of the helicopter, he ran toward the ditch, leaping in right behind Jahm Shedi. They had barely made it to the ditch when the helicopter exploded with a sudden billowing of fire and smoke.

Five minutes earlier

As they were leaving Even'song, John had seen the helicopter. At first he paid no attention to it. Then he saw it make a sharp, spiraling descent.

There was really no way to explain how he knew,

but he knew. Perhaps there is some truth to the belief that those who live their entire life on the edge develop a sixth sense. Although there was nothing to suggest it, and no reason to suspect it, John knew as surely as he knew his own name that the helicopter would be waiting around the bend for them. When he voiced his opinion to the others, they accepted his warning without question, for they too knew the value of such intuition.

John stopped the car, then put one rock beneath the accelerator to prevent it from being depressed all the way, and another on top of the accelerator in order to make it go forward. The road was slightly banked around the curve, and John was counting on that to keep the car on the road long enough for his plan to work.

With their weapons in hand, the three cut through the dogleg. They came out onto Breeze Tree Road on the other side of the hovering helicopter at about the same time the car was taken under fire. As the car exploded, John stepped out into the middle of the road behind them, knowing that the attention of everyone in the helicopter would be directed toward the burning car.

John started firing at the tail rotor, aiming at the center of the spinning disk. As he hoped they would, the bullets hit the pitch-change links. Unable to adjust the pitch on the tail rotor, the pilot could no longer maintain control. The helicopter began spinning wildly, shot up about twenty feet, then came crashing back down.

Ahmed lay in the ditch, looking back toward the road, his weapon at the ready. Smoke from both the burning car and the helicopter swirled around him, and the air was redolent with the smell of burning jet fuel, oil, rubber, fabric, melting metal, and human flesh. Because of the great temperature generated by the fiercely burning helicopter and car, Ahmed's vision was distorted by undulating heat waves. The world itself had taken on an ethereal mien. He could see John on the other side of the flames, but the heat was bending the light so that John appeared to be floating, ghostlike, across the ground.

"No!" Ahmed shouted. Climbing out of the ditch he started running toward John, firing as he ran. At almost the same moment, those rounds remaining in the helicopter started cooking off, and they streamed out in every direction from the burning wreckage like the ejected bits of color from a fireworks starburst. John belly flopped onto the ground to avoid being hit, but Ahmed wasn't as lucky. Three of the rounds hit him and he went down.

By the time the last round cooked off, Jahm Shedi had climbed out of the ditch and was standing on the road with his hands up, begging John not to shoot, shouting that he was a hired pilot, not a hired gun.

Ahmed was still alive, though barely. John hurried to his side.

"You are a devil, John Barrone," Ahmed said. "You are the spawn of Satan, sent to test me." He coughed, and blood flecked at his mouth, indicating a punctured lung. "I failed the test," he added.

"Who are you?" John asked.

"You do not remember me?"

"No."

"David Bin-Yishai did not remember me either. He died never knowing why he was killed."

"You were there," John said. "You were the one who killed the woman hostage, the one who got away."

"Yes."

"John?" Jenny called to him. Jenny was standing just on the edge of the ditch, holding the little canvas bag. She held up two videotapes she had taken from the bag.

"What are they?" John asked.

Growing Wheat in America's Breadbasket is one; the other is *The Mississippi Delta, America's Rice Belt.*"

"You have to be kidding me."

"Watch them," Ahmed said. "I think you will find them very interesting. I'm sure the devil Quinncannon enjoyed the one I sent him."

"It was you?" John asked, surprised by the revelation. "You are the one who sent Quinncannon the tape of his granddaughter being killed?"

"Yes," Ahmed answered. "And I hired the studio to make that film, using his granddaughter. I wanted to make him pay in tears for the blood he caused my people to spill."

Ahmed tried to laugh, but it came out as a hacking, blood-spewing cough. That changed to a gasp for breath. Then he was quiet.

John watched as Ahmed's eyes glazed over with death.

FIFTEEN

Wet Spot Productions

Tony Sarducci's personal office rivaled the office occupied by any of the executives of the major film companies. It was sixteen hundred square feet of opulence, complete with two bathrooms, a wet bar, and a teak desk as large as the bedroom of some small apartments. In one corner of the room, a twelfth-century Persian carpet set aside a section on the myrtle-wood floor to be used as a seating area. There, a leather sofa and two leather chairs were grouped around an elaborately hand-carved coffee table. The walls were decorated with movie posters, from *Birth of a Nation* to *American Beauty*. Interspersed among the recognizable movie titles were several little-known pictures, such as *Glory Dust, The Last Raid,* and *When Honor Dies.* Though the latter pictures had been produced by Sarducci, they were not Wet Spot productions, nor were they even X-rated. They were what, in the old days, would have been called B pictures, and today, small-budget, independent creations.

Tony Sarducci stood at the wet bar, pouring a lime-colored liquid from a beaker over cracked ice in salt-rimmed goblets. He brought one of the goblets over to Frank Giles. Giles was program director for the Cosmos Cable Network. As such, he had the responsibility to acquire properties for next season's schedule. He had called Sarducci this morning to ask if he could come over to talk about *Beach Vice.*

"Here you go," Sarducci said, handing the drink to Giles. "A perfect margarita. As far as I'm concerned, this is the only thing worth a shit that Mexico ever produced."

"Oh, I don't know. I like Mexican food," Giles said, accepting the margarita.

"Tex-Mex maybe. Real Mexican food is inedible." Sarducci sat on the chair, across from Giles. "So, you are interested in *Beach Vice?*"

"It's one of several shows I'm considering for next year," Giles said. He leaned back in his chair and wrapped his fingers around his drink, like a cardplayer covering his hand.

"Well, I have to tell you, if you want it, you had better act quickly. I think ABC is about to make an offer. And HBO wants it for a series. I'd really like to go to HBO with it because we'd have a lot more freedom there." He laughed. "We could even show a tit or two."

"Quite frankly, Tony, your 'showing a tit or two,' and much more, is one of the things that has raised some concern over at Cosmos."

Sarducci looked surprised. "What do you mean?"

"I'm talking about your company Wet Spot Productions," Giles said. "We like to consider our network a network for the family. To be honest, *Beach Vice* is already a bit of a stretch, what with all the skimpy bikinis and the suggestive story lines. Add to that the fact that it is a Wet Spot Productions show and . . ."

Sarducci waved his hand. "You don't have to

worry about that, Frank. Wet Spot Productions is something I came up with just for the adult films. I'd be using Parasail Pictures for *Beach Vice*. And, of course, any other general pictures I might do."

"That's not enough," Giles said. "We would have to have your word that you are no longer involved with Wet Spot Productions."

"I have no problem with that," Sarducci said. "Wet Spot was a necessary evil, put into operation only to save my studio. But I would much rather be making more traditional pictures. Hell, I'll close Wet Spot down today, in fact."

"If we can have that guarantee, I think we can create some wonderful entertainment for our viewing audience," Giles offered.

"You have my guarantee," Sarducci replied.

"I've already shown the pilot film to my people, and they agree that it has a certain quality, an ensemble appeal like some of the more successful shows in the business. We are ready to sign an agreement for thirteen episodes for this coming season. We'll give the show a prime slot and a lot of network hype. In short, we will do everything in our power to make it a success. Do you think you can get into production quickly enough to meet that schedule?"

Sarducci smiled broadly. "I'll have half of them done by premiere week," he said.

"And you'll tell ABC and HBO that the deal is off the table? I mean, once we start serious negotiations, we don't want you playing tag with anyone else."

"I'll call them today," Sarducci promised. He smiled. This would be an easy promise to keep. Both ABC and HBO had already turned him down.

"Well, then, I'll go back and tell my people we are going to do some business," Giles said.

"You won't be sorry," Sarducci replied, shaking Gile's proffered hand.

Sarducci walked to the front door with Giles, then, after Giles left, practically danced back to Wanda's desk.

"Did it go all right?" Wanda asked.

"All right? It was great! Wonderful! Stupendous! Wanda, my dear, we are back in the business, the *real* business. No more making pictures for dirty old men wearing raincoats. This time next year, we'll be in the hunt for an Emmy."

"Oh, Mr. Sarducci, I knew they couldn't keep you out of the business forever."

"What do we have in production now?" Sarducci asked.

"*School for Sex* is in edit and *Coed Sex Club* is set to start next week."

"Cancel them. Cancel both of them," Sarducci said with a wave of his hand. "And get in touch with the distributors, tell them that Wet Spot is no longer in business. Then call the writers who worked on *Beach Vice* and tell them to be here at Parasail Pictures tomorrow for story conferencing."

"Parasail?"

"Yes, Wanda. Wet Spot is dead. Long live Parasail."

Sarducci started back toward his office. Just as he got to the door he turned back toward Wanda. "Oh, and call the decorators and sign people. See how fast they can convert the studio back to what it once was."

"Yes, sir!" Wanda said happily.

Sarducci returned to his office and poured himself another margarita. He sat down behind his desk, put his feet up, and took a sip. As of this moment, he was on top of the world.

Suddenly, and without a knock, the door was pushed open and Natas stormed in. He slammed the door behind him, then crossed the floor with a purposeful stride.

"What's this shit Wanda is saying about closing the studio?" Natas asked.

"We're not closing the studio. We are only shutting down the adult-film business. Didn't Wanda tell you the whole thing?" Sarducci grinned, broadly. "It's wonderful news, Natas! We are going to do *Beach Vice* for the Cosmos Cable Network. Ha, I'm going to have to start hitting some of the 'in' places again, reestablish some old contacts. I knew I'd get back in the game some day."

"Have you lost your mind? You're giving up a gold mine just so you can go back and hobnob with all those Hollywood assholes?"

"It's more than that, Natas. I don't expect you to understand. I know I never was a very big player in this game, but when I was doing my movies, even movies like *Night Train to Yuma,* I had some respect."

"Respect, my ass," Natas said. "You were lucky to get a hundred screens. Your pictures were a laughingstock. Nobody respected you."

"At least I got screens. And it didn't matter whether I had anyone else's respect or not. I had my self-respect."

"Yeah, well, when you came to me crying that the bank was going to take everything if you didn't come up with half-a-million dollars, you didn't have much self-respect."

"I know," Sarducci said. "I didn't think I could sink any lower than I was then. Of course, that was before I found out about your 'special projects' division. Child pornography. May God forgive me for that, because I will never be able to forgive myself."

"That's very touching, Sarducci," Natas said. "But I would like to point out to you that just one kiddie-porn picture makes more money than five of the others."

"There is more to this business than money," Sarducci said.

"Yes, so you said. There is self-respect." Natas laughed, though his laugh was without humor. "You forfeited any self-respect you ever had when you came to me for help."

"Just because I slipped down into a pit of depravity doesn't mean I have to stay there."

"Oh, but I'm afraid it does," Natas said. "Have you forgotten? My associates and I own forty-nine percent of your company."

Sarducci smiled. "Yes, less than half. That means I still have control."

"No, you also have forty-nine percent. Wanda has two percent, and she'll be voting with us."

"Don't be ridiculous. Wanda has been with me for more than twenty years. Do you think, for one minute, that she will vote with you?"

"She already has," Natas said. "I'm sure you are aware that Wanda has a gambling problem. I helped her out of a little jam with the ponies a few months ago. In return, she has given me an irrevocable assignment of proxy to vote her stock."

"I'll buy her stock," Sarducci said. "A stock transfer will revoke the proxy."

"I want to ask you one more time to consider what you are doing," Natas said. "Think about it, Sarducci. Why, I'll bet if truth were known, you are making more money now than three fourths of the movie and network people in this town."

"I already told you, money isn't everything."

"And there is nothing I can do to change your mind?"

"Nothing."

Natas was silent for a moment. Stroking his chin, he studied Sarducci through narrowed eyes. "How much do you know about our special films division?" he asked.

"I know as much as I want to know," Sarducci replied. "When I found out you were making films using underage actresses, I told you that I didn't approve, and you agreed that I was to be kept out of it."

Natas chuckled. "Yes, I think the politicians call that procedure 'plausible deniability.' It would be interesting to see if that defense would really work. Are you prepared to put it to a test?"

"So, what are you telling me, Natas? That you intend to blackmail me with a few child pornography pictures? I was never on the premises when any of those pictures were being shot. I'll swear they were all done behind my back, and without my permission or knowledge. And you know what, wise guy? I still have enough friends in this business that I will be believed."

"You may get a wink and a nod on the kiddie porn," Natas agreed. "But not on the other thing."

"The other thing? What other thing?"

Natas chuckled. "You know, I am really going to get a kick out of this, Sarducci. I mean, when you consider the irony of it all. Like you said, you just might be able to beat the child pornography rap. But nobody is going to let you get away with the other thing, even though you really didn't know anything about it."

"*What the hell other thing are you talking about?*" Sarducci shouted.

Natas pulled a videotape cassette from his jacket pocket and held it up. "I think it's time to show you one of our XSM pictures."

"XSM?"

"Extreme Sadomasochism. After you have seen it, you may decide that it wouldn't be prudent to rock the boat."

"I doubt it. There is absolutely nothing you can show me or tell me that will make me give up my chance to get back into legitimate production," Sarducci insisted.

"You may be right. It could be that you have more guts than I think you do," Natas said as he put the tape in the player. "I suppose we'll see, won't we?"

"Satan Productions," Sarducci said, as the opening credits began to roll. "I never did ask you. What made you come up with a name like that?"

"It's Natas backwards. Didn't you realize that, Jaybez Stone? You made a bargain with the devil, and no Daniel Webster to defend you." Natas laughed out loud.

"You are sick," Sarducci said. "Anyway, I don't have anything to do with this, and I never have."

"Of course you do, Sarducci. You are the producer of record of every picture Satan has done."

"*Oval Orifice?*" Sarducci asked as the picture started. "Is this what you are planning to show me? If you remember, when we first made this picture, the girl swore that she was of age. She even had a driver's license that verified her claim. Besides, this picture has already been pulled out of circulation. You can't frighten me with this."

"Oh, but I think I can frighten you. You see, this

is a very special edition of *Oval Orifice,*" Natas said. "One you haven't seen. We revised the ending. As a matter of fact, why don't I just get to it so you can see what I'm talking about?"

Natas stopped the tape, then ran it fast-forward. When the tape started slowing down, indicating that it was getting near the end, Natas punched "play" again.

"Here it comes," Natas said. "Tell me what you think."

A few minutes later, Wanda passed Sarducci in the hall as he was heading for his office.

"Mr. Sarducci, I spoke with the writers. They are very excited, and they will be here to—oh, Mr. Sarducci, you don't look well. You don't look well at all. Are you all right? You look as if you have seen a ghost."

Sarducci walked right by without answering her. Wanda would have thought that uncharacteristically rude of him had she been sure he saw her. The funny thing was, even though they passed within inches of each other, she could almost swear that he hadn't even seen her.

Sarducci closed the door to his office. Wanda started toward it, not only to tell him about the writers, but to make certain he was all right. In all the years she had known him, she had never seen him like this.

She heard the lock click.

"Mr. Sarducci?" Wanda called, now a little anxious about him. She knocked on the door. "Mr. Sarducci, why have you locked the door? Are you all right?"

Natas came out of the back part of the studio,

and saw Wanda standing just outside Sarducci's door.

"Mr. Natas, I'm worried about Mr. Sarducci. I've never seen him looking so—"

The sound of the gunshot was so loud and so startling that Wanda wet her pants.

Sunset Motel

Don found the story right after they returned to Los Angeles. It didn't make the front page; it didn't even make it above the fold on page sixteen. But it was news they found interesting.

ADULT-FILM MAKER COMMITS SUICIDE

Anthony J. Sarducci, 43, took his own life Wednesday afternoon, shortly after three o'clock. Wanda Carmody, a long-time associate, stated that he went into his office at Wet Spot Productions, 9220 Palm Avenue in Burbank, and locked the door behind him. A moment later, she heard a shot. When she, Anton Natas, vice president of Wet Spot Productions, and Alfred Rodl, chief of security, broke the door open, they found Sarducci dead at his desk.

Sarducci left no notes. Friends and associates are puzzled as to why he took his own life.

"He was very excited about the prospect of doing a show for the Cosmos Cable Network," Ms. Carmody stated, though Frank Giles of Cosmos would not confirm that they were in the process of closing a deal.

Anton Natas said that Wet Spot will continue doing adult films. "It was Tony Sarducci's dream to make adult films that could compete, artistically, with the more traditional films. I intend to dedicate myself to fulfilling that idea."

Natas said that *School for Sex*, Wet Spot's next release, would be dedicated to the memory of its founder and president.

"So, what drove our man over the edge?" Jenny asked after all of them had read the news article.

"Maybe he thought we were getting too close," Don said.

"Maybe he thought he was going to get a deal with Cosmos, and when it fell through, he couldn't take it," John suggested.

"You really believe a scumbag like Sarducci thought he had a chance at something like that?" Jenny asked.

"As a matter of fact I do," John said. "I remember that he told me how close he had come to getting a series. I think, at heart, he considered himself a real filmmaker. The adult-film business was something he got into just for money."

"It's hard to believe someone who was really legit would make kiddie porn just for money," Jenny said.

"Yes, well, that's another thing. Sarducci was noticeably uncomfortable with the concept of child pornography."

"You mean frightened that he might get caught?"

"No, I mean uncomfortable as in, he didn't really want to do it."

"Wait a minute. Are you defending him? After all he did?"

"I'm beginning to think we may have been going

down the wrong path. I have a feeling that Natas is the one we are really interested in."

"All right, so what's next?"

"I think it's about time Sal Todaro paid Wet Spot Productions another visit," John suggested.

Wet Spot Productions

"You idiot, that's John Barrone," the big man said, looking at the videotape Natas had taken from the security camera. "What was he doing here?"

"He said he was in the business, looking for kiddie-porn tapes. But you know what? Now that I think back on it, I believe that even from the beginning I knew there was something fishy about him," Natas said.

"He's after more than kiddie porn.

"You mean the XSM projects?"

"XSM," the big man said, scoffing. "Call them what they are, you perverted little prick. They are snuff films."

"You have no right to call me perverted. We are painted with the same brush," Natas said. "You are as involved in this as I am."

"Oh, no, my friend. There is a big difference between us. I am in this just for the money. And if we off a few street whores, who the hell is going to miss them? As far as I'm concerned, we're doing society a favor. But you, you perverted little maggot, you get off on it."

"There is nothing wrong with a person enjoying his work," Natas said defensively.

"You make me want to puke," the big man said. He nodded toward the security tape. "Just stay away from this man. Otherwise, you could bring us all down."

"Oh, shit," Natas said. "He called this morning, wanting another appointment. That's when I decided to call you and see what you thought about it."

"Did you make the appointment?"

"Yes. I guess I can call and back out of it."

"No, wait," the big man said, holding his hand up. "I've got an idea."

"What sort of idea?"

"Keep the appointment. This might be just what we are looking for."

"Are you going to kill him, like you did the others?"

"Yeah, if I have to. But I'm going to have to give this a little more thought. So far, nobody gives a shit about anyone I've killed: the whores, the pedophile, those two kiddie-porn peddlers. If you will notice, not even the news media shed tears over any of them. But we may not be that lucky with Barrone."

"Who is he anyway? Is he with the police?"

"I'm sure he isn't local police. But I don't really know who, or what, Barrone is. All I know is, he has some very powerful connections. And if something happens to him, there would be a lot of shit come down."

"Well, when he shows up I could play dumb, pretend I don't know what he's talking about."

"No, don't do that. I have an idea. You say he's been asking about kiddie porn?"

"Yes. He claims he's some big distributor, says he can make us a lot of money."

"He's running a scam, trying to get some evidence on the operation here. I tell you what. When he shows up today, give him a couple of kiddie-porn tapes."

"What? That's what he is here to find, isn't it? Why should I make his job any easier for him?"

"Because sometimes you have to set the trap. Give him those tapes, then, as a decent citizen, make a call to your friendly Vice cop." The big man smiled. "That would be me," he added. "And that will be all the excuse I need to take care of him."

"He'll just get out of it," Natas insisted.

Sergeant Wallace shook his head slowly. "No, he won't. Not as easily as you think he will. Once a man gets a sex offender tag hung on him, it stays with him, whether it is justified or not. Hell, I'll probably get a citation for shooting the son of a bitch."

SIXTEEN

When John entered the office, he looked toward the receptionist's desk expecting to see Wanda Carmody. Instead of the attractive, middle-aged woman, he saw the brutish chief of security, Alfred Rodl.

"Where is Wanda?" John asked.

"She don't work here no more," Rodl said.

"That's too bad. She added a bit of class to the place."

"What do you mean?"

"Never mind."

"You here to see Mr. Natas?"

"Yes."

"Wait here, I'll call him," Rodl said, picking up the phone.

"Where would I go?" John replied easily.

Within a minute Natas came through the door that led into the back. He was smiling effusively, and he stuck his hand out toward John. "Good to see you again, Mr. Todaro."

Natas's handshake felt exactly as if someone had put a dead fish in John's hand.

"Come back to my office," Natas said, swiping his card through the electronic lock. John followed him into the back, beyond the line of smaller offices, then into a very large office at the end of the hallway. He had never been in this office before, and was somewhat surprised by its size and opulence.

"I was saddened to read about Sarducci," John said.

"Yeah, well, like they say, shit happens."

"So I've heard."

"He did it right here, you know," Natas explained, almost as if he were giving a tour. "Got blood all over this desk. Didn't know if I was going to be able to get it all out or not. I had to work like hell to clean it up. But it was worth it to move in here."

"This was Sarducci's office?"

"Yes."

"Very impressive. I've not seen it before."

"He was pretty vain about it, didn't let just anyone in. But I like to think he would want it to be used."

"I'm sure he would," John replied. "Why do you suppose he did it?"

"What? You mean, why did he eat a bullet?" Natas shrugged his shoulders. "Who the hell knows? It was a total surprise to everyone who knew him. But then I don't guess anyone ever really knows what is going on inside another person's head."

"I suppose not," John agreed. "I take it, however, that Mr. Sarducci's unfortunate demise won't interfere with our business?"

"No, not at all. In fact, it might even make our business easier," Natas answered. "Ever since Cosmos Cable started talking to Sarducci about doing a show for them, he started having second thoughts about doing adult films. *Any* adult films, and especially the ones we are doing in our special films division. But I intend to carry on, and I guarantee you, Mr. Todaro, you will be pleased with what we can supply you."

"You do remember my requirement, Mr. Natas. No one is to know of our working arrangement. I hope you haven't spoken of me to anyone."

"Mr. Todaro, you asked us not to check you out with anyone else, so I didn't. In this particular line of the film business we don't have the protection of copyright, or contract, or anything like that. Our word is our only bond. You understand that, I'm sure."

"Of course," John said.

Natas opened one of the desk drawers and pulled out two videotape cassettes. "I tell you what I'm going to do. As a token of trust, I am going to give you these two tapes. They are representative of our special films division. Look them over. If you like what you see and you still want to do business with us, I think we can make you a very good deal." Natas put the two tapes into a padded envelope and taped it shut, then handed the envelope to John.

"Thanks," John said. "I'll get back to you very soon." He held up the tapes. "And I look forward to previewing these."

"By the way, I would be very careful of those tapes if I were you," Natas called to John as he started to leave. "Not for my sake, but for yours. These tapes are so hot that even possession could get you ten years in prison."

John was about two blocks away from the studio when a car pulled up behind him. The car's headlights began flashing alternately, left, right, left, right, while red and blue lights winked out from behind the grill. It was an unmarked police car.

John pulled over to the side, kept his hands on the steering wheel, then looked in the mirror as the policeman exited his own car. He was surprised to see that the policeman who stopped him was Sergeant Larry Wallace, the Vice cop from Lieutenant Jackson's station.

"You doing traffic now, Sergeant Wallace?" John asked. "I'm pretty sure I didn't violate any traffic regulations."

"You want to step out of the car, Mr. Barrone?" Wallace replied in a very intimidating, very official police voice.

John exited the car as directed.

"Would you put your hands on the top of the car and spread your feet, please?"

The way Wallace delivered the question indicated that he wasn't really asking, he was telling. Once John had assumed the position, Wallace began tapping him down. After a preliminary inspection, the policeman stepped back with a surprised look on his face. "You aren't carrying heat?"

"Just because I have the authorization to carry a weapon all the time doesn't mean I do," John replied.

"What about the car? You have a weapon in the car?"

"No," John said.

"You don't mind if I look, do you?"

John glanced back on the front seat of the rented Ford. The padded envelope was lying there in plain view. He thought of what Natas had told him as he left the studio, how the tapes were so hot that unauthorized possession could get him up to ten years in prison. And though he was involved in an investigation, he had no official sanction; therefore he had no protection against such possession.

"Do you have a warrant?" John asked.

"No."

"Well, then, if it is all the same to you, I'd rather you not look through my car," John said.

Wallace smiled. "Oh, I'm sure you would rather I not search. You have something to hide, don't you? Step away from the car, please."

"Are you placing me under arrest, Wallace?" John asked.

Wallace pulled his pistol and pointed it at John. "I said step away from the car," he repeated, more forcefully this time. He made a waving motion with his pistol.

John moved away, as ordered.

Wallace sniffed at the open window of John's car, then smiled triumphantly. "Whoa," he said. "I do believe I smell marijuana. I guess I won't be needing that search warrant after all, will I? It would appear that I have reasonable suspicion."

"That's lame, Wallace, and you know it," John said. "You don't smell marijuana. And you have insufficient cause for reasonable suspicion. So if you do search my car, no matter what you find, it won't hold up in court."

"No matter what I find? And just what is it I might find?" Wallace asked. "What are you worried about? That I might find some kiddie porn?"

"Kiddie porn? Now, why would you suspect I might have kiddie porn?"

"I have a tape of you attempting to buy video tapes showing children engaged in sexual activity."

"Is that so? How did you come by such a tape?"

Wallace chuckled. "Interesting. You aren't trying to deny the existence of the tape. You are just questioning how I got it. This tape came from Wet Spot Productions' surveillance camera."

"I can explain the surveillance film," John said. "I was operating undercover when I tried to buy those tapes. I'm on a case."

"A case for who? Private? State? Federal? Just who are you, Mr. Barrone, and what are you doing here?"

"I told you, I am conducting an investigation. What are you doing here, Wallace? And how did you manage to get that tape?"

"It was given to me by my business associate."

"Your business associate?"

"Yes. Perhaps you know him. Anton Natas?"

"My God, you are doing business with Anton Natas?"

"It seemed like the thing to do," Wallace said.

"And here I thought you were on such a crusade to clean up the world."

"Clean up the world? Don't be naïve, Mr. Barrone. The world can't be cleaned up, it doesn't want to be cleaned up. I couldn't beat it, so I joined it. Since that time, Natas and I have had a most profitable relationship."

"What about Sarducci?"

"Sarducci was a gutless coward," Natas said. "There is no doubt in my mind I was going to have to take care of him sooner or later. By offing himself, he just saved me the trouble."

"What about Annette Quinncannon."

"What about her? She's dead."

"How do you know she's dead? Have you found her body?"

"She's dead," Wallace said again, without elaboration. "You know what I think, Barrone? I think you are a chicken hawk."

"A what?"

"A chicken hawk. I'm sure you've heard the term. It refers to someone who likes to get it on with kids. But the thing is, most of you perverts can't get it up, so you have to get your kicks by watching kiddie porn. That is right, isn't it, Mr. Barrone? You aren't really looking for Annette Quinncannon, are you? You know as well as I do that the Quinncannon girl is dead."

"Do I?"

"If you haven't figured that out yet, you aren't much of a cop." Wallace looked into the car. "Well, now, what do I see here? It appears to be a padded envelope. And I'll just bet if I opened that envelope, I would find two kiddie-porn films. Would you like to take that bet?"

"I never bet against a man who has gone to all this trouble to set something up," John said.

Wallace chuckled. "You think I set this up, do you? Well, we'll see what a judge thinks." Wallace reached down into the car and picked up the envelope. "Two kiddie-porn tapes. That ought to be worth about ten years in prison, don't you think?"

"I never think about such things," John replied.

"No, I wouldn't think you would. But ten years is the penalty for having something like this," Wallace said. He stuck his hand into the envelope.

Maybe it was something in the way Natas had couched his warning as John left the studio. Whether it was that, or John's sixth sense kicking in, he'd thought it better to be safe than sorry. As a result, he had removed the two cassettes Natas gave him, put them under the seat, then replaced the cassettes with a couple of paperback books.

"What the hell?" Wallace spouted in surprise as he pulled out the two paperback novels. "What is this?"

Wallace looked up to question John, but John wasn't there.

"Barrone!" Wallace shouted, enraged that John had disappeared, right before his eyes. "Barrone, where are you, you son of a bitch?"

"I'm over here," John answered quietly. While Wallace was distracted by the envelope, John had slipped, quickly and unobserved, back to Wallace's car. He was now standing just behind the open door. "What do you say we call for some backup?" he suggested, holding up the microphone to Wallace's police radio.

"Get away from that radio!" Wallace shouted. Suddenly, and without warning, Wallace began firing. John leaped into the car, then rolled over into the backseat, thankful that this was an unmarked car and not a cruiser, which would have had the backseat caged.

The bullets from Wallace's .44 Magnum penetrated the door as easily as if it had been made of paper. With a frustrated yell, Wallace adjusted his aim, firing into the car. One of his bullets punctured the radiator, sending a spew of steam into the air. The other bullets smashed through the windshield, front seat back, second seat back, and punched out through the trunk deck.

Reaching up to the weapons holder just above the window, John grabbed the shotgun, then rolled out of the back door and onto the ground. Sticking the barrel of the shotgun under the car, he aimed at Wallace's feet, then pulled the trigger.

"Ahhh!" Wallace screamed as his feet were shot out from under him. He crashed down to the ground, then, seeing John through the bottom of the car, managed to squeeze off one more shot. This shot hit the tire right beside John. A high-pressure jet of air blew in John's face as the tire began deflating rapidly.

John fired back. Because Wallace was lying on the ground, he took the full brunt of the shotgun blast. Wallace's face turned to red hamburger meat as he dropped his gun. His head fell forward and John knew, without having to check, that the man was dead.

In the distance, John could hear the sounds of approaching emergency vehicles. Getting up, he ran quickly to Wallace's body, retrieved the padded envelope, then got into the rented Ford and drove away, still carrying the shotgun he had used to kill Wallace. Three miles down the road John tossed the shotgun through the open car window into a creek. He knew full well that the gun would be found soon, but he knew also that the stream would wash away his fingerprints and that was all that was important to him.

The whole thing had been a setup. Natas had wanted to smoke John out, but the plan had backfired. Instead of smoking John out, it had exposed Sergeant Wallace as a dirty cop.

It had, however, closed the door to any future undercover operation as far as John was concerned. On the other hand, it tended to confirm what John had only suspected to this point. Wet Spot Productions, and in particular Anton Natas, had produced the two snuff films he had seen. John didn't know if there had been any other snuff films produced, but he knew for a fact that there wouldn't be any more. He would make sure of that.

SEVENTEEN

The Oriental visitor who stood in the lobby of Wet Spot Productions was carrying a satchel and a long cylindrical case. He wore an ill-fitting suit and square-toed shoes, and had poorly cut hair. His horn-rimmed glasses were fitted with exceptionally thick lenses. As a result, the almond-shaped eyes in his round face were greatly exaggerated.

Nervously, the visitor extracted a cigarette from a Japanese package, then lit it. He held the cigarette between the ring finger and little finger of his right hand, smacking his lips somewhat as he pulled the cigarette from his mouth. As he exhaled, he blew out a tight stream of the very strong, acrid smoke, looked at his watch, and tapped his foot nervously.

Natas and Rodl were in Natas's office, watching the nervous actions of their unexpected visitor on a closed-circuit security monitor. The fact that the subject didn't realize he was being televised made the close inspection all the more telling.

"What did he say his name was?" Natas asked as he watched the man on the screen.

"The name he gave me was Yutake Yamaguchi," Rodl answered.

"Yutake Yamaguchi," Natas repeated. "That's a Japanese name, isn't it?"

"Jap, yeah. He said he was a customer of Mehdi al Ahmed. A 'special' customer is the way he put it," Rodl added.

"Special?"

"That's what he said."

"That sounds to me like he is trying to give us a signal," Natas said. "Have you ever seen him before?"

"No," Rodl said. "You want me to run him off?"

"I don't know," Natas said. "If he's real, we can't afford to run him off. Ahmed was our biggest customer and he brought in a lot of money. Now that he's gone, we need to start looking for another market. If this man was a customer of Ahmed, he might be just what we are looking for."

"But we don't know anything about this guy," Rodl insisted.

"Well, look at him, for chrissake," Natas said. "How bad can he be? I mean, he looks like a gardener or something."

As they continued to observe him via the security camera, the visitor took off his glasses and wiped the lenses with his handkerchief. When he did so, he squinted his eyes until they were bare slits. After he finished cleaning his glasses, he put them back on very carefully, slipping them over one ear at a time.

"I'm going to see what he has to say," Natas said.

The visitor smiled broadly, and bowed slightly as Natas came out to greet him.

"*Ohio*—" the visitor started to say. Then he laughed with embarrassment and covered his mouth with his hand. "You will excuse, please, that I started to greet you in my own language. I now greet you in the English. To you the day is good, Mr. Natas."

"Good day to you, Mr. Yamaguchi. What can I do for you?"

"Excuse, please?"

"Why are you here?"

Yamaguchi smiled, then bowed slightly. "Ah, yes. For the movie I am here. You will please give to me now?"

"What movie?"

The visitor looked surprised for a moment, then laughed. "Oh, I see. It is a joke you make. Yes, is very funny. What movie." He held up his finger and waved it back and forth. "Yes, very funny."

"Mr. Yamaguchi, I am not trying to make a joke," Natas said. "I don't know what the hell movie you are talking about."

The smile left the visitor's face. "Mr. Natas-san. One-half million dollars already have I given you. The other half million with me to this country I have brought." He opened the briefcase, and Natas gasped because it was filled with large stacks of one-hundred-dollar bills. "Two hundred fifty thousand now, and the rest when you deliver *Shattering of the Crystal* to my hotel room. Here is a card from the hotel. It is as we agreed, yes?"

Natas and Rodl looked at each other in confusion; then Natas spoke.

"Now who is playing the joke?" he asked. "I don't know anything about any film called *Shattering of the Crystal*. And I especially don't know anything about the half-million dollars you say you have already paid."

The visitor looked shocked. *"Shattering of the Crys-*

tal you have not made? What have you done with the money?"

"I told you, I don't know anything about the money," Natas said.

The visitor hit the top of his head with the heel of his hand.

"Oh, my," he said. "Forgive me for the stupid I am. Perhaps Mr. Ahmed died before he could give you the money."

"Either that, or he kept your money," Natas said. "All I know is, it never got to me."

"Then I must give you one thousand apologies. How embarrassing this is." He put his hands together and bowed.

"What type of film is *Shattering of the Crystal*?"

"When one dies at the peak of one's beauty, my people refer to it as the 'shattering of crystal,'" the visitor said. "The market for such a film, the death of a woman at the height of her beauty, would be small, but most appreciative and most rewarding."

"You are talking about a 'special' film?" Natas asked.

"Yes. I believe you call them, what is the term? Snuff films."

Natas held up his hand quickly, interrupting his visitor. "That is not a term one throws around," he said. "You would be better off forgetting you ever heard such a term."

"Ah, yes, of course. But when I speak of a special film, this is what I mean. In the past, I have bought such films from Ahmed. Now I will buy from you. Or have I made the mistake? Perhaps you're not the ones who supplied Ahmed with his films."

"We were Ahmed's supplier."

"And will you now deal with me? Or has the confusion over the money caused a problem?"

"No problem, Mr. Yamaguchi. I'm sure we can work out some arrangement, just as I am sure we already have a film that will fit your special, uh, needs."

The visitor shook his head. "No, I am certain that you do not. You see, for it to be a true shattering of the crystal, the woman must be of a more mature age than anything I have seen in your films. She must be at the peak of her beauty. In my culture, that occurs between the ages of thirty and forty. Our crystal goblet must be Caucasian, tall, blond, very nice, uh . . ." He put his hands in front of his chest.

"Titties?" Rodl asked.

The visitor nodded enthusiastically. "Yes, titties," he said. "Tall, blond, big titties, and between thirty and forty years old. In the final scene, the crystal is to be shattered by use of an ancient Japanese sword. The sword is very old and very, very valuable. It is said to be a twelfth-century sword of the Mikado."

"Where is this sword?" Natas asked.

"I have it here." He opened the long, cylindrical case and extracted a sword. The blade flashed brilliantly in the ambient light of the lobby.

"Ayyyyyiiieeee!" he shouted, whipping the sword around over his head, then making a slash at Rodl.

"Hey!" Rodl shouted in alarm.

Smiling, the swordsman held his hand out and opened it up. He had sliced through Rodl's bushy eyebrows, cleanly severing a hunk of hair.

"I think you will agree that the sword will make a most beautiful instrument with which to shatter the crystal."

"Yes, I can see that it would. But Mr. Yamaguchi, I'm afraid we have a problem," Natas said.

"What is the problem?"

"You say you have already paid half-a-million dollars? Well, we haven't received half-a-million dollars, and I tell you quite frankly, there is no way I am going to make this movie unless I get all the money, including the money you say you gave Ahmed."

"I understand," Yamaguchi said. "And I apologize if I did not make myself clear. Of course, I will pay all the money you have coming to you."

"There is another thing," Natas said. "This business about having a woman between thirty and forty years old?"

"Yes."

"Well, that might present a problem as well. You see, the women we use in these, uh, special films are prostitutes that we take from the streets. That way nobody misses them, nobody cares if they are gone. But we can use only the younger ones, because by the time they are as old as you want, they are wasted and ugly."

"I am sure you can find someone who is suitable."

"It isn't going to be as easy as you think," Natas said.

"Perhaps another two hundred fifty thousand dollars will make your search easier. A total of one million, two hundred and fifty thousand dollars I will pay if, to me, you will give the film I want. And if you let me watch."

"Wait a minute, you want to watch?"

"Yes."

"Impossible. When we do one of these special pictures, the set is closed."

"Too bad." He closed the briefcase, picked it up, and started toward the door. "Perhaps I can find someone else who will accept my money."

"Wait!" Natas called as his visitor started to leave. The visitor stopped and looked back.

"I think we can work something out," Natas said.

"You will let me watch?"

Natas nodded, then stuck out his hand. "Mr. Yamaguchi, you have a deal," he said.

"When?"

"Go to your hotel and wait. We will let you know."

"Very good. I will wait with much eagerness."

John and Jenny were having lunch in John's motel room when Don came in.

"Did you save me any lunch?" Don asked when he saw them eating.

"There's another hamburger and some fries there," John said, pointing to a McDonald's sack. "But we figured you would eat before you came back."

"I did," Don said easily. He unwrapped the hamburger and took a bite.

"So, how did it go?" Jenny asked.

"You're right about one thing, John. Shaking hands with Natas is like grabbing hold of a dead fish."

"So you met him?"

Don put the hamburger down and put his hands together, prayerlike, under his chin. He squinted his eyes into narrow slits, then bowed his head.

"The honorable Yamaguchi-san made a deal with the honorable Natas-san for the shooting of the film *Shattering of the Crystal*," Don said, speaking in a heavy accent.

"Damn if that isn't about the best impression of a Japanese I've ever seen a Chinese do," John said, laughing at Don's impersonation.

"Hey, how would you know the difference?" Don

replied. "To you Caucasions, all we Orientals are the same."

"Well, that's true," John agreed. "The big question is, did he take the bait?"

"Did he take the bait?" Don replied. "If I had hooked him on a two-hundred-pound test line, I would have reeled him in."

"Okay, Jenny, the next move is up to you," John said.

"Right."

"Be careful, okay?"

Uptown Morris laid out two lines of coke on a silver platter, then rolled up a one-hundred-dollar bill. He sniffed up both lines, then looked over at Natas. The end of Uptown's nose was dusted with a residue of white powder. The white powder highlighted the wounded nostril.

"That is some premium shit, my man. Premium shit," Uptown said about the coke.

"What the hell happened to your nose, Uptown?" Natas asked.

Natas put a hand up to the wound, then glared. "I had a little accident," he said.

"It looks like shit," Natas said.

"Yeah. Well, it ain't nothin' I can't handle. So, what you comin' to me for?"

"Mr. Morris, I have a requirement which only you can fill."

"Call me Uptown, my man," Uptown said.

"Yes, Uptown. I have come to you a few times in the past for some special needs, and you have been able to furnish them. For that, I thank you."

"And so now you got another one of them needs, right?"

"Yes."

"It's goin' cost you twenty thousand."

"Twenty thousand? You've only been charging fifteen thousand."

"Right now, I ain't go no ho's that's givin' me a bad time. I been givin' you only them ho's that was givin' me a hard time," Uptown explained. "Bunny, Sheeba, and them other two. And one of 'em that you done, that bitch Tulip, didn't even come from me. Man, can't see why you done her. That was a waste, man."

"Tulip didn't belong to you."

"So now, if you wantin' another ho' from me, you goin' have to pay twenty thousand dollars. 'Cause after you snuff 'em, they gone, man. They can't never bring in another dollar for ole Uptown."

"You asked for twenty?"

"Yeah, man. Twenty."

"I'll give you thirty thousand dollars," Natas said.

Uptown blinked a couple of times, pinched the end of his nose, then blinked again.

"What you talkin' 'bout?" he finally asked.

"I'm talking about thirty thousand dollars. I'm going to give you thirty thousand for the next one you bring me."

"What's the catch, man? I can't see you payin' me no thirty thousand dollars lessen they's somethin' bad connected to it."

"No catch."

"No catch, huh? Okay, I'll bring you one tonight."

"No catch," Natas repeated, "but there is a requirement."

"Oh, so there's a re-*quire*-ment," Uptown said, dragging the word out. "Okay, so now we down to the nut-cuttin', is that it? What is this re-*quire*-ment you talkin' about?"

"It can't be one of your regular whores," Natas said. "This one has to be special."

"Yeah, well, no problem, man, I got one bitch that is prime. You know what I mean? Big brown eyes, skin so gold it shine, this girl be fine. Only problem she has is her mouth. She don't never keep it shut. I been thinkin' I need to take care of her. This will do it."

"No," Natas said. "She won't do."

"Why? 'Cause she black? You got a bunch-a redneck, cracker honkies 'fraid maybe if they jerk off while watchin' a black girl, some of her color goin' get on 'em?"

"They aren't honkies," Natas said. "They aren't even white, but the woman they want in the film has to be white."

"That's okay, I got plenty of them too."

"And over thirty," Natas added.

"Say what? You tryin' tell me you got some people wantin' to watch some thirty-year-old broad gettin' whacked?"

"Not just any thirty-year-old," Natas said. "She has to be blond, beautiful, and well shaped."

Uptown snorted. "Man, you tell me they ain't no catches to this, then you say the woman has to be over thirty and pretty. You know how many ho's still look good when they're that old?"

"Not very many, I'm sure."

"Not very many," Uptown said. "You want somebody who still good-lookin' when they that old, you got to go outside the profession. Ain't no ho' that old still lookin' good, less they just come into . . ." Uptown paused in mid-sentence. Suddenly he snapped his fingers and smiled. "Damn, I know where one is. She be an uppity bitch too. I'll be glad to see her get what's comin' to her."

"Is she a whore?" Natas asked. "She has to be a whore. I don't want anyone to come lookin' for her."

"She's a ho', all right," Uptown said. "Only thing is, she didn't start whorin' till just a few weeks ago, so she's still fresh. Almost a virgin, you might say."

"How old is she?"

"Between thirty and thirty-five, I'd say."

"And pretty?"

"Right now, I'd say she's the prettiest bitch on the street."

"If she's all that, why are you letting her go?"

"You can't let go of somethin' you don't have," Uptown said. "I tried to talk to this bitch, tell her that she need to come with me, and all I get from her is a little sass and back talk. Well, I can't put up with that, you know what I mean? I gotta let all the rest of my ladies know what happen when you try and cross ole Uptown." He put his hand to the wound on his nose.

"Is she the one who did that to you?" Natas asked, pointing to Uptown's nose.

"Yeah," Uptown said, stroking it gently. "I'm really goin' to enjoy this job."

"Don't mess up her face. If her face is messed up, the deal is off."

"You don't worry none about that," Uptown said. "She'll be as pretty when I hand her to you as she is right now."

Jenny Barnes examined herself in the mirror. She had put glitter in her blond hair, her eyebrows were plucked and arched, and her lipstick was so glossy she could practically see her reflection. Her breasts were spilling out of the half-cup push-up bra, her midriff was bare, and she was wearing a red G-string, wide-mesh red hose, and white plastic high-heel boots that came up to her knees.

"Damn, woman," John teased when she came out of the bathroom. "You're in the wrong business. You could've made a ton of money selling your ass."

"Screw you and the horse you rode in on," Jenny snapped back. She caught her reflection in the mirror. "I look like a whore," she said.

Don laughed.

"What is so funny, Mr. Yee's number-one son?"

"You are *supposed* to look like a whore," Don said.

Jenny laughed. "Yeah, I guess I am. You like my outfit?"

"Well, I wouldn't recommend that you wear it to a PTA meeting, but it does have its points," John said.

"Yeah, maybe more than you think," Jenny replied. "It looks like it's made of shiny plastic, doesn't it?"

"There is a certain gaudiness to it, yes," John agreed.

"It is plastic, or rather, plastique. It is all pure C-4 plastique explosive. I'm wearing enough punch to take out a medium-sized dam." She reached back to adjust the butt strap of her G-string. "But explosive or not, when this thing goes up your ass-crack, it can be very uncomfortable."

"Yeah?" John teased. "Keep telling yourself that, kid. I wouldn't want you to suddenly find yourself enjoying this."

Jenny grabbed a glass off the dresser and threw it at John. It zipped by his head, barely missing, then smashed against the wall behind him.

"Whoa!" John said, holding his hands out in front of him. "I give up!"

"You damn well better," Jenny said.

"All right. Don, you need to get back to the hotel in case they try to get in touch with you," John said. "By the way, Jenny, with all the explosives you are wearing, where is the detonator?"

"It's right here, behind my G-string, riding comfortably against my crotch," Jenny said.

"Damn! That's a hell of a place for a detonator," John said.

"Yes, well, if this thing goes off prematurely, I want one last thrill," Jenny teased.

John laughed. "You are some piece of work, you know that?"

"Of course I know it," Jennie answered easily. "Hell, I've always known that."

"René? René, is that you, girl?" Dawn asked shortly after Jenny arrived on the street.

"It's me," Jenny answered.

"Hey, girl, you lookin' good!" Dawn said. "What have you done to yourself?"

"A little touch-up here and there and some new clothes is all," Jenny said. "I was getting tired of being left behind every night."

Dawn chuckled. "Who you think you're kiddin'?"

"What do you mean?"

"You a fine-lookin' woman. You got that kind of classy look that lots of men like. If you been left behind, it's cause you wanted to be left behind."

"No, really I—"

"Hey, look, ain't no one blamin' you, girl. I mean, you got that nice gig with the rich man's son. Hell, I'd be hangin' back hopin' for somethin' like that to happen again myself," Dawn said.

For a moment, Jenny was confused. Then she remembered that Sheeba had told the others that she had spent the weekend on a yacht with the son of a very wealthy man.

"Yes, well, now you know my secret," Jenny said. "But I've about decided those kinds of gigs only come along once in a blue moon. So, if I'm going to make a living, I'm going to have to peddle my ass just like everyone else."

"You got that right, girl," Dawn said. She looked at Jenny's exposed rear end, then chuckled. "And you sure advertisin' the wares," she added.

"You think it's too much?" Jenny asked, sticking her butt out.

"I always say if you got it, show it. And honey, you sure got it," Dawn said.

Rock Hardon was more than a porn star. He was also the computer wizard who had designed Satan Production's Web site, complete with all the encrypted protections. It was through the Web site that they advertised their unique offerings, and through the Web site that they checked out potential customers.

Shortly after Don Yee, posing as Yutake Yamaguchi, left the studio, Natas asked Rock to find out everything he could about him. Rock spent almost two hours on-line, subjecting Yamaguchi to an exceptionally thorough investigation.

In the corner of his motel room, Don was eating a Twinkie and watching the screen of his laptop computer. He knew that Natas was going to have Yutake Yamaguchi checked out. Because Natas had a very sophisticated Web site, Don was fairly certain that the investigation would take the form of an Internet check, either by Natas himself, or by whoever it was that designed the Web site.

Don had created a virtual sniffer, a means of alerting him whenever anyone, anywhere on the Net, initiated a search for Yutake Yamaguchi. Then, once he determined an inquiry was being made, he was able to activate the inquiry, to actually read the questions. In that way, he could supply the answers he wanted the snooper to have.

A spyglass icon suddenly popped onto his screen.

"Hello," Don said aloud. He pushed the rest of the Twinkie into his mouth until his cheeks actually bulged. A few keystrokes took him to the source of the inquiry. The screen name of the intruder was DvlsAcolyte.

In the search box, DvlsAcolyte typed *Yutake Yamaguchi.*

Don had already preloaded the responses, and he overrode the search engine with his own responses, marked "1 through 727." For the first response he had written: *Yamaguchi, Yutake, underground Japanese filmmaker, best known for the offbeat and bizarre. Specialty is in films depicting sexual perversions.*

As Don knew he would, that was the response the computer researcher selected. From that point on, Don led the researcher through a series of inquiries, carefully constructing the persona of a non-existent person.

"Served five years in Nogata Prison for possessing and selling drugs. Has been tried, but never convicted, for possession of sexually explicit films which exceed the Japanese Moral Code for film.

"Has private account in Swiss bank."

After Don played cat and mouse with whoever was trying to discover information on Yutake Yamaguchi, the Internet intruder withdrew. He was very careful not to leave any notice of his intrusion.

Don removed the second Twinkie from its wrapper and stared at the screen as the intruder very carefully covered his tracks. Within seconds, there would be no sign that anyone had ever been inquiring about Yutake Yamaguchi. The intruder did that by implanting a very dedicated worm. The worm destroyed all the evidence of his entry.

"Oh," Don said. "You are good. You are very, very good." He opened a sack of Cheetos, grabbed a handful of the little orange bits, and stuffed them into his mouth. He reached for a Coke, unconcerned that it had already reached room temperature. "Yes, sir," he said as he washed all the Cheetos down with several long swallows of Coke. He pulled the can away, then wiped his lips with the back of his hand. "You are damn good, but I am better."

"He checks out okay," Rock Hardon told Rodl.

"You sure?"

"I'm positive," Hardon said. "He has been all through our site, ordering some very interesting items. Then, about six months ago he connected with Ahmed, and since that time, was clearly Ahmed's best customer."

Hardon had given his report to Natas and Rodl. After listening to it, Natas stroked his chin for a moment; then he looked at the other two. "You know what I'm thinking?" he asked.

"Don't have any idea," Rodl answered, even though the question was rhetorical.

"I'm thinking that if we are going to make this picture for Yamaguchi, why not make about three more at the same time? With four of them made and in the can, we'll have enough money to walk away from here before anyone ever gets wise to us."

"You want to do four pictures at the same time?" Hardon asked.

"Sure, why not? We aren't exactly making *Gone With the Wind* here."

"Easy for you to say," Hardon said. "I'm the one who is going to have to get it up every time."

"I'll get Bruce to help you."

"Wait a minute," Rodl said. "Bruce doesn't know anything about the snuff films. Do you want to take a chance on him finding out?"

"Not much of a chance," Natas said. "There's nothing that says we couldn't snuff Bruce."

"What would you think about that?" Rodl asked Hardon.

"Wouldn't make any difference to me."

"But I thought you and he were . . ."

"Were what?" Hardon replied. "In love?" He laughed. "As far as I'm concerned, he's just another pretty young boy. I use them and throw them away like old condoms."

"We'll snuff him," Natas said easily. "A picture where a homo gets snuffed might open up a whole new market for us."

EIGHTEEN

When the deep purple Cadillac with a gold Rolls Royce grille stopped at the curb, the girls around Jenny became nervous.

"What's Uptown want now?" Dawn asked.

"I don't know, but it won't be good. Nothing good ever happens when he comes around."

"If you all feel that way about him, why do you use him?" Jenny asked.

" 'Cause we got no choice. And if you plan on livin' much longer, you'll figure out pretty soon that you got no choice either."

Three doors opened on the Cadillac, and Uptown and his two bodyguards jumped out. They started toward Jenny, and she moved onto the balls of her feet to get ready for them.

"Ain't none of that karate shit goin' help you this time, girl," Uptown said. He put his hand under his jacket, and when it came out, he was holding a pistol. His two bodyguards also pulled pistols. "We got three guns on you," he said.

"What do you want?" Jenny asked.

A broad smile spread across Uptown's face. His gold tooth flashed. "Well, now, ain't you the helpful one? What do I want? I want you to get in the car, that's what I want."

"Why would I do that?"

Uptown pulled the hammer back on his pistol. The sear engaged the cylinder with a deadly-sounding double click.

"Get in the car, bitch," he said. "Or I'll blow you away right where you stand."

"Uptown, you got no right," Dawn said, but Uptown turned his gun toward her.

"You want to die first?"

"No, no," Dawn said, holding her hands out in front of her as if, that way, she could ward off the bullets.

"Then shut the hell up. My business is with this bitch." He turned the gun back toward Jenny. "I'm goin' count to three. If you ain't movin' toward this car by the time I get to three, you one dead piece of ass. One, two—"

Jenny started toward the car.

"Well, now, that's more like it," Uptown said.

The big white bodyguard opened the rear door and motioned with his hand for Jenny to get in. Jenny did as she was directed.

The car was as gaudy inside as it was outside. The seats were rolled leather, lavender in color. The carpet was pink. The dome light was a tiny chandelier.

"Nice car," Jenny said, looking around. "Who did your decorating? Liberace?"

"Who?" the black bodyguard asked.

"Never mind, it's a joke."

"You ain't in no position to be making jokes," Uptown said as he started the car. He was silent for a moment. Then he laughed.

"You think of a joke?" Jenny asked.

"Yeah," Uptown said. "What's going to happen to you. That's a joke."

* * *

Don was occupying a four-room suite in the Academy Arms, one of the most luxurious hotels in Hollywood. The Academy Arms was owned by Marist Quinncannon, an irony that wasn't lost on Don. He was expecting a telephone call from Natas, and was just finishing a bowl of vanilla ice cream, topped with strawberries, chocolate syrup, crushed nuts, and whipped cream, when the doorbell rang. It startled him, because he still wasn't used to a doorbell in a hotel suite. Setting the bowl aside, he walked over to open the door, expecting to see John. He was surprised to see Rodl.

"Natas sent me," Rodl said.

"I thought you were going to call me."

Rodl shook his head. "It is better this way. Besides, if I called, you would never be able to find the place."

Don forced a laugh. "I know how to find the studio."

"Yeah, well, that's the thing, you see. We don't do these pictures in the studio."

"Where do you do them?"

"I'll take you there," Rodl answered.

"I'll just get my—" Don started.

Rodl interrupted with a shake of his head. "You are to bring nothing with you," he said.

"Money," Don finished. "Does Natas-san not want his money?"

"Money? Let me see it," Rodl said.

Don unsnapped the briefcase and opened it, displaying, one more time, the neat stacks of one-hundred-dollar bills. "Here it is," he said.

Rodl looked at the money, then nodded. "You can bring it," he said.

"And the sword?"

"Yeah, but maybe you'd better let me carry the sword," Rodl suggested.

Don pointed out the sword, then closed his briefcase, snapped it shut, picked it up, and followed Rodl out the door.

When the phone didn't answer after several rings, the hotel operator came on the line.

"I'm sorry, sir, your party does not answer."

"Would you let it ring a few more times? He's probably in the bathroom or something."

"There is a phone in the bathroom," the operator replied. "I'm sorry, he isn't answering."

John hung up, then drummed his fingers on the desk for a moment. He realized then that they must have made contact with him. Don wouldn't leave until he heard from them, and if they had called him, Don would have called John. They must have come to get him.

Don wasn't the only one missing. By agreement, Jenny was to call in every hour as well, but she'd missed the last hour, and it was almost time for another check-in. If she didn't check in this time, John was sure it would mean she had made contact.

Of course, John could contact Jenny, but it might be risky. Even if she had her pager on vibrate, if he chose an inopportune time, it could cause trouble for her. John decided not to wait anymore. He would go to the studio himself.

It had grown dark by the time John pulled in to the studio parking lot. The studio appeared to be deserted. Even the gate shack at the parking lot was empty. John parked as close to the studio buildings as he could get, then left the car.

He had come prepared for a nighttime incursion. He was dressed in black from his head to his feet, complete with hood. Strapped to his belt was a small black bag, filled with specialty items that would make his mission easier. With pistol in hand, he moved through the shadows to the nearest window. It took him less than thirty seconds to open the window and crawl inside.

John took a pair of night-vision glasses from his bag, thus allowing him to negotiate the dark hallways and passages. He explored the entire building in less than five minutes. The building was empty.

In order to be present for the filming, Don had agreed to be blindfolded. After a ride of some thirty minutes, the car stopped. Don sat there for a long moment, listening to the silence. Overhead, he could hear an airplane. The airplane's engines were in acceleration mode, so he knew they were climbing. That meant he was upwind of an airport, but which airport? LAX? John Wayne? In the distance, he could hear a train.

"You can take off your hood," Rodl said.

Don removed the hood and looked around. He found himself in a warehouse district, with literally hundreds of over-the-road trailers parked, some backed up against loading docks, others sitting on dollies.

"In there," Rodl said, pointing to the building in front of them. Like many of the other buildings, this one had trailers backed up against the loading dock. As Don passed close by the trailers, he saw that their dollies were dry and rusted and the wheels were weeping grease. This was evidence that they had been motionless for a long time. It made a perfect cover.

Natas met Don just inside the door of the warehouse.

"Welcome to Satan Studios," Natas said, taking in the building with a wave of his hand. "Not quite as glamorous as Wet Spot, but as you can see, we have everything we need to get the job done."

Don saw light racks and camera stands. Most of the lights were focused on a stage that was set as a bedroom. Don saw three young women, bound and gagged, sitting in straight-back chairs, watching everything through frightened eyes.

"Who are these women?" he asked.

"Don't worry, they don't have anything to do with your film," Natas replied. "I thought that, as long as we were setting up for one picture, we might as well do four."

"Where is the woman for my picture?"

"She'll be here," Natas said. "In the meantime, you can watch us make the other pictures."

"No!" Don said sharply.

"What?"

"You must do my picture first."

"Why?"

"Because no one can die before the crystal is shattered. And that includes those women."

"They don't have anything to do with your picture. I don't understand what your objection is."

"I do not expect the Western mind to comprehend," Don said. "It is like the elegance of a single bloom, as compared to a large bouquet. I must insist that no one else die. Should it happen, it would destroy the exquisite beauty of a single death."

"All right, all right, if you are that determined, we'll do your picture first," Natas said.

Their conversation was interrupted then by several voices coming from the front of the building.

Natas smiled. "Well, Mr. Yamaguchi, I do believe your 'crystal' is here."

Don saw four people appear from the shadows at the front of the building. One of the four was Jenny. "What the hell is going on here?" Jenny asked.

"Do you find her satisfactory?" Natas asked Don.

"Oh, yes, she is lovely," Don replied.

"Who's the Jap?" Jenny asked. "Is that what this is all about? You brought me here to screw a Jap? Well, hell, I'd as soon screw him as anyone else. What do you say, Mr. Moto, are we going to get it on?"

"Must she talk?" Don asked.

"Uptown, please advise your client not to speak unless spoken to," Natas said.

"Shut up, bitch!" Uptown said.

Don started toward the briefcase.

"Where you going? What you doing?" Natas asked anxiously.

"I am keeping my end of the bargain," Don replied. He pointed to the briefcase. "I am going to get the money for you."

"Rodl will open the case," Natas said.

Don said nothing, but he watched Rodl, trying in vain to open the case.

"I can't get it open," Rodl said.

"I have it locked."

"Tell him the code numbers," Natas ordered.

"One, four, one, four," Don said.

Again, Rodl tried, without success, to open the case.

"You do it," Natas said.

Don nodded, then walked over to the case and turned the four locking wheels.

Three miles away, the GPS presentation in John's car suddenly came alive. In the middle of the presentation was a series of red concentric circles. "Way to go, Don!" he said, throwing the car into a sliding 180-degree turn. Ignoring the honking horns of irritated motorists, John accelerated to seventy miles per hour as he started toward the spot indicated on the GPS locator.

"Get your clothes off," Natas said to Jenny.

Without hesitation or embarrassment, Jenny began stripping. She removed her bra, dangled it in front of Uptown, then dropped it at the foot of a support girder. Then, parading in front of all of them with an exaggerated sway of her butt, she stopped by another girder, lifted a shapely leg, and slid off her boot. Throwing her hip to the side, she twirled the boot a few times, then dropped it.

Once again, she began parading across the floor.

"What the hell is going on here?" Natas asked. "You think you are Gypsy Rose Lee or something? Just take off your damn clothes and be done with it."

"No, wait!" Don said. "Before the crystal is shattered, it must shine. Please, allow her to do this."

"Yeah," Rodl said. "I'm sort of enjoying it myself."

Next, Jenny walked over to Uptown and hooked

one leg around him. She began grinding herself against him.

"What you think you're doin', bitch?" Uptown asked.

"Uptown, baby, I just want to show you what you'll never have," Jenny said. She put her hand down inside his trousers and grabbed him, giving him a little squeeze.

"What you doin' grabbin' me like that, woman? You showin' me what I can't have, or feelin' up what you can't have?" Uptown asked, laughing out loud. His two bodyguards laughed with him. Jenny removed her last boot and dropped it near Uptown.

Now, wearing only her G-string, she paraded to the middle of the floor. There, undulating like a snake, she stripped out of the G-string and wrapped it around the center post of the warehouse. Now completely naked, she stepped out into the middle of the floor, threw her arms over her head, spread both legs, and thrust her pelvis forward.

"Okay, honey, I'm all naked, hot and ready," she said. She looked at Don. "Bring on the little Jap. Do you want me to do him in front of everyone?"

"Rock, get ready," Natas said.

"I'm ready," Rock replied, coming toward them. Like Jenny, he was totally naked. Behind him, Bruce was sitting on the floor with a somewhat fanciful look on his face, as if proud of himself for getting Rock ready for his performance.

"Rodl, you and these two go out front. Keep an eye open," Natas said.

"I want to watch," one of Uptown's guards said.

"Go," Uptown ordered. He smiled. "I'll watch for all us. I'll tell you what it was like."

Grumbling, the two guards joined Rodl out front.

"What are we doing out here anyway?" one of the guards asked. "We're in the middle of nowhere. Ain't no one goin' to come out here."

"Just do it," Rodl ordered.

The three men had just taken their positions at the front when one of them thought he saw something. "Who's there?" he called.

"What is it, George? What do you see?" Rodl asked.

"There! By the trailer!" George called, pointing toward John, who, in his black outfit, was barely visible. George opened fire.

"I see him!" Rodl cried, and he too began firing.

With bullets ricocheting off the side of the trailer, and making fireballs on the concrete around him, John dropped to the ground, then rolled behind the set of dual wheels and began returning fire. He saw one of the men go down.

"Let's get out of here! It's the cops!" Natas yelled. He started to run, but Jenny spun around and kicked him in the side of the knee, sending him sprawling.

Hardon grabbed Jenny from behind, and putting his arm around her, twisted her neck, trying to break it. Don came to her rescue, hitting Hardon in the temple with the heel of his hand. Hardon went down.

Suddenly bullets started whistling by both Don and Jenny's head as Uptown opened fire on them. Jenny dived one way, and Don went the other.

The firing out front stopped. "Jenny! Don!" John shouted, running into the building. "Where are you?"

"Rock, let's get out of here!" Natas shouted.

Uptown fired another long burst, forcing Jenny and Don to keep their heads down, while at the same time affording Natas and Hardon the opportunity to escape.

"Wait!" Uptown shouted, running back into the shadows after Natas and Hardon. "Wait on me, you bastards!"

With Uptown chasing Natas and Hardon, Jenny and Don were able to regain their feet. John arrived at that moment.

"Are you both okay?" he shouted.

"Yes," Jenny replied. "But they're getting away."

"Natas! You son of a bitch! Open this door!" It was Uptown's voice, echoing through the cavernous interior of the warehouse, edged with fear and rage.

"Well, two of them are getting away anyway," Jenny said. She grabbed a pair of cut-off jeans and a T-shirt from a wardrobe rack and, within seconds, had covered her nudity. That was when she saw the three women for the first time. All three were handcuffed and gagged. Their eyes were wide with terror.

"Holy shit, where did you come from?" she asked. She removed their gags, and they all started talking at once.

"Never mind, never mind, just get the hell out of here," Jenny said as she untied them. "Run, don't look back."

All three women ran, and Bruce, who had been hiding in the shadows, jumped up and ran with them. John swung his gun toward Bruce.

"No, John, no!" Don yelled. "Let 'im go, he's nobody."

Suddenly several flashes of light, accompanied by the crashing sound of gunfire, erupted from the back of the building as an enraged Uptown was spraying gunfire all around.

"Let's get after Natas," John said.

"What about *him?*" Don asked, pointing in the direction of Uptown.

"Don't worry about him," Jenny said. "He'll be taken care of when the building goes down."

"You've got the charges planted?" John asked.

"Yes, let's get out of here. Natas and Hardon are getting away."

As the three ran out of the building, Jenny reached over and grabbed a video camera. They ran across the parking lot until they reached John's car.

"This ought to be far enough," Jenny said. "I'm going to set off the charges."

"How are you going to do that?" Don asked. "I didn't see you plant the detonator."

"Sure you did," Jenny replied with a smile. "You saw me put it right between Uptown's balls."

"What?"

Jenny took a garage opener from the visor of John's car and pointed it at the building. She pressed a button and, a second later, the inside of the building erupted with several flashes of light, clearly visible through the windows. The light was followed by a rumbling roar, then a fiery burst, and finally a large puff of smoke. The warehouse collapsed in on itself, exactly like the controlled demolitions of those downtown buildings that were razed when a city underwent renovation.

They heard a squeal of tires; then Don saw the car. "That way!" he shouted. He started to get behind the wheel, but Jenny grabbed him and pulled him away.

"No way am I going to get in a car chase with you driving!" she said, pushing him into the backseat. She climbed into the front seat with John, who, even as Jenny was shutting the door, had the car started.

With smoke streaming from the tires, John pulled onto the road behind Natas and Hardon. There was very little traffic, so they were able to close the distance quickly. Jenny saw a wink of light from the right window of the car ahead; then the right outside mirror shattered.

"They're shooting at us," Jenny said.

John began swinging the car back and forth in a series of S turns. That prevented the people ahead from getting a shot at them, but it also caused them to lose some ground.

Natas pulled onto the I-5, then accelerated to over one hundred miles per hour. Only the fact that it was late and traffic had thinned prevented a sure collision. As it was, the car ahead snaked in and out of traffic, sometimes passing on the right shoulder, other times moving all the way over to the left shoulder to pass. John stayed right on his tail.

Suddenly Natas came all the way across the highway, barely missing several cars, to crash through an exit ramp that was blocked by a CLOSED barrier. John, Jenny, and Don made the turn right behind them. To everyone's surprise, the road led out onto what was going to be an overpass, but the overpass was incomplete and it ended abruptly, some one hundred feet in the air.

John saw Natas's brake lights come on, and smoke pour out from all four wheels. John slammed on his own brakes, coming to a halt just behind Natas, who managed to stop just inches short of going over the edge.

John eased up behind them, then stopped.

"Shall I?" he asked.

"Do it," Don said.

"Wait," Jenny said. She picked up the video camera she had taken from the studio, then moved up even with the front door of Natas's car. Natas looked toward her, an expression of confusion on his face.

"Ready . . . slate . . . action!" Jenny shouted.

John moved up until his bumper was against the back bumper of Natas's car, then began pushing.

Natas suddenly realized what was happening to him.

"What the hell are you doing?" he shouted, putting on the brakes. When that didn't help, he shifted quickly into reverse and pressed hard on the accelerator. His back wheels began spinning in reverse, sending smoke churning up from the screeching tires. But the inertia was with the rear car, and Natas realized, in horror, that he was going over. He looked over, one more time, toward Jenny, who, with the camera, had moved right up to stand inches away from the open window.

"Smile, you son of a bitch," Jenny said. "You are about to be snuffed."

Both Natas and Hardon screamed and threw their arms across their faces, just as the car went over. Jenny hurried to the edge of the overpass, still filming. Her viewfinder captured the car plummeting downward, flipping upside down, and growing smaller as it descended until finally it hit the ground far below. There was a puff of dust and a grinding crash of metal, then a blossom of flame, followed by the heat, shockwave, and stomach-jarring thump of an explosion.

Two days later,
Even'song Estate

John, Jenny, and Don reported to Marist Quinn-cannon that Anton Natas was dead. They told him that the police theorized that he had run into financial difficulties with his movie studio, committed suicide by driving over the edge of a half-completed overpass, with his homosexual lover and porn star, Rock Hardon, at his side.

"Here is a videotape you might want to see sometime," John said, handing Quinncannon the tape Jenny had made of Natas's last few seconds. "We couldn't bring Annette back to you, but I can promise you that there will be no more young girls who suffer the same fate. At least, not from Anton Natas."

Fighting back the tears, the old man nodded in appreciation. It wasn't the perfect closure, but under the circumstances, it was as close as he could get.

THE *CODE NAME* SERIES
By William W. Johnstone

Today, when bomb-throwing madmen rule nations and crime cartels strangle the globe, justice demands extreme measures. For twenty years, ex-CIA agent John Barrone fought his country's dirty back-alley wars. Now, he spearheads a secret strike force of elite law enforcement and intelligence professionals on a seek-and-destroy mission against America's sworn enemies.

Be sure to order every book in this thrilling series from the master of adventure, **WILLIAM W. JOHNSTONE . . .**